Guide Wars

JOHN HOLT

ILLUSTRATIONS
BY PARKS REECE

Wilderness
Adventures
Press

Gallatin Gateway, Montana

Wilderness Adventures Press books are made to last for generations. They are printed on acid-free paper that will not turn yellow with age. The bindings are Smyth-sewn, allowing the books to open easily. Our binding boards are covered with 100% cloth. We commission today's top sporting artists to illustrate our books. We believe that our books are the finest sporting books published.

Second Printing

Published by Wilderness Adventures Press
P.O. Box 627
Gallatin Gateway, MT 59730
800-925-3339

10 9 8 7 6 5 4 3 2

Printed in the United States of America

Library of Congress Catalog Card Number: 97-061437

ISBN 1-885106-43-2 Trade; 1-885106-44-0 Limited

For John Talia

"Enough to eat and...a little more
than enough to drink; for thirst
is a dangerous thing."

Jerome K. Jerome
Three Men in a Boat

Table of Contents

Acknowledgements

Without the kindness and understanding of the many guides, including Jack Mauer, I fished with over the years, there would be no book. Thanks to Tim Joern for showing me how to use a new machine, Tony, Bob, Jake, Ginny, Jack, Elizabeth, and Rachel…and to Mom, who has always been there.

Introduction

THERE AREN'T MANY TIMES when the fishing is this good or this easy, for that matter. The river and its healthy population of powerful rainbow trout were in fine form during a late September float. The sky was cloudless and the temperature hung out around 80, normally poor conditions for catching fish but of little consequence today.

A small dry cast 30 feet or so from the raft turned trout at almost every riffle, current seam, or deep run. Small pheasant-tail nymphs were just as productive. The fish took the patterns deliberately, then raced fast, fast, fast downstream, quickly running into our reels' backing. Even smaller rainbows of 14 or 15 inches turned the trick, and all of them leaped and crashed across the glassy surface of this central Montana river.

This was a stretch of river I'd not worked before. I'd driven by the water many times on my way somewhere else. The idea of finding this kind of quality action had never crossed my high-speed, pile-down-the-road mind before. Like so many trips before this one, I had a guide to thank for another joyous outing on the water. And, to a large extent, that's what guides are for. That's what they are paid for, but that's just part of the story. There's so much more.

If there's one axiom I've formulated concerning fishing with guides, it's that good guides are worth the price of admission and bad guides are hell on earth.

To begin with the latter first, a bad guide thinks that he is the only individual with the skill and experience to fish properly. Anyone else is a rank beginner who belongs somewhere else, certainly not in his boat. How these happy individuals justify this attitude while accepting a check from their clients is something of a mystery. Bad guides are convinced that they could show the likes of Lee Wulff or Lefty Kreh a thing or two. Every cast you make, every knot you tie, every fly you select, the way you play a fish—all of this is done improperly, sloppily, without skill according to a bad guide. And these cheerful souls will let you know their feelings, either through constant verbal abuse or by a disposition that is at once sullen and ice cold.

Many years ago, while fishing the Madison River below McAtee Bridge, I had the distinct pleasure of spending a very long day in a drift boat with an individual whose idea of guiding was, first, to show up hung-over (not always a fatal flaw as we shall see later) and an hour late. After 30 minutes of rigging up and listening to this guy run down the quality of my equipment, we set sail. On my first cast, he made his position clear.

"What in the hell was that? You'll put down every god-damned trout in the river," he politely offered as the hopper hit the water. Seconds later a nice rainbow rose to the offering, and I quickly worked the fish to the boat. The guide grabbed the leader and shook the startled fish free and said, "Worse case of playing a trout I ever saw."

The day grew worse, and I was nearly terminal velocity as far as my temper goes. I was so angry I lost what little casting coordination I possessed and began to live up to this clown's expectations. Lunch was the ubiquitous balogna sandwich and warm pop, consumed in stony silence. The rest of the afternoon was more of the same until I somehow hooked a decent brown that raced across current and broke off on a midstream boulder. The guide went ballistic.

"Son-of-a-bitch. Work my ass all day to put him into fish and he blows it. Bullshit. That's enough."

I lost it at that point, turning around from my perch in the front of the boat and wholeheartedly agreeing with this boy's opinion. A few other things were said and violence was looming on the near horizon. The guide rowed to shore, hopped out of the boat, and stomped downstream to smoke in ugly solitude. I grabbed my gear, walked up the rise to the highway and hitched back to my car. I left a check, sans tip, for the day's delightful adventure on the dash of the guide's battered pickup —cracked windshield, bald tires, ratty seats, rusted-out body (actually, this sounds a good deal like what I'm driving today). I was tempted to let the air out of his tires, but there were too many people in the lot to make this a wise proposition.

Admittedly, that is the worst day on the water with a guide that I've ever endured, but there have been others of similar constitution. Like I said, bad guides are hell—pure misery. They should be keelhauled—immediately, if not sooner.

On the other side of things, there are those guides (and they are the vast majority) that make a day on the river into something special—magical and memorable. Like the day mentioned at the beginning of this—a time that could have lasted forever as far as I was concerned. The guy knew the water and the flora and fauna with the skill of a trained biologist. He was kind, helpful, encouraging, and possessed a wealth of strong opinions that he tempered naturally with a subtle sense of humor. In other words, he was a professional and a decent human being.

I've always wanted to write a book about guides—the good and the bad. Both need the recognition they deserve. The following nine stories are fiction only in the sense that I've changed the names of the people involved, have taken a certain degree of license with linear time for the sake of narrative, and allowed my imagination to run its course.

For the pros out there on the water laboring under trying conditions, dealing with difficult clients or stubborn fish, and doing so with a smile and a well-tempered sense of determination, there's always a cold beer in my cooler or a splash or two of whiskey in my flask. For the bastards like the Bozo on the Madison, may a wind-blown, heavy-weight, #2 woolly bugger lodge deeply in your ear lobes.

O·N·E

Wasted Away on the Gulf

IF YOU ARE FROM MONTANA AS I AM, even the relatively benign sun of a late March Florida afternoon seems intense. Early spring or the end of winter (take your pick) in the northern Rockies is normally drab, dreary, cold and wet, and usually quite muddy. These uncomfortable conditions are only slightly ameliorated with the knowledge that warmer weather and sunny skies will arrive shortly—say by early July. So 90-degree heat and a harsh sun beating down on me, and also beating back up in my face as the light ricochets off the clear, glowing blue water's surface, is at once pleasant and a bit tough to take.

Bonefishing attire is a humbling but necessary exercise in woefully poor taste. My own attire consists of a garishly-colored jade shirt, awful green baggy pants, and a hat with a long spoon bill and a long floppy flap that wraps around my ears and neck like a low-priced Billings hooker. Every surface still exposed to the sun, and there are few, is drenched in oily sunscreen with an SPF of something around 4,000. It's so hot, I'm beginning to feel like the main event at a pig roast. An unpleasant experience, but fortunately, a steady breeze makes all of this bearable.

Henry, my guide and dear friend, is poling our flat-bottomed boat through shallow water of three or four feet in search of redfish and maybe a bonefish or two. Having obviously dealt with hundreds, maybe thousands, of hapless fools from up north trying to cope with similar ailments, he is unconcerned with my discomfort. He wears nothing but a ragged pair of cutoffs, white T-shirt, battered Florida Marlins baseball cap, and a pair of wrap-around sunglasses. His skin is baked to a deep brown, so much that I wonder if melanoma heaven awaits somewhere in his glistening future. Other guides down here who I have talked with are now, to some extent, limited in their time on the water due to sun-inflicted skin cancer, but not Henry, who could be 40 or 60. He's talkative only on a few subjects, namely the best bars to pick up women, "dumb-assed tourists," and a fervent love of rum with ice and lime juice.

We have not seen any bones, as this is not the best water here south of Boca Grande, and it is too early for most of the tarpon that have carved out a niche in local island history over the decades due to their numbers, size, and incredible fighting abilities. But we are running across good numbers of redfish that are holding in barely discernible depressions in the sandy bottom. They average 10 to 12 pounds, and Henry calls them "puppy drums." I've been told that they can run to over 80 pounds, but nothing in that heroic range will be found this far south. All the same, a 10-pound fish that takes my small (by saltwater standards) 1/0 crab imitation (providing I don't scare the hell out of the fish with one of my numerous errant and windblown casts) is a pleasant reprieve from the noisome atmosphere swirling around Montana right now.

Even in my hideous attire, the fishing is great sport. Dressed like this in south Chicago I'd either be dead in a minute or auditioning for a part in some overhyped episode of ER. I guess how I look does not really matter way out here on these isolated miles of sand flats. Ragged jeans, beat-up fishing shirt, and moldering tennis shoes are all I wear up north, anyway. Why care down here?

"Over there, Holt. How blind are you anyway?" Henry asks with a cough laced with the gravel of last night's rum and a pack or two of Camel straights. I followed the direction of his extended hand and soon saw a dark shape 40 feet away, motionless. Whipping a quick cast well ahead of the fish, the crab sank and I twitched the thing slightly a few times, moving the pattern closer to the fish that languidly moved out of its "hole" and sucked in the fake. Setting the hook did not provoke any water walking or airborne heroics, but rather a long, steady run aimed for the sanctity of the deep blue water several hundred yards distant.

The strength of the redfish was amazing. The thing just kept going, pulling line off the reel and stirring up tan-white clouds of sand with its tail. I finally checked the thing, not through any skill or artifice on my part, but rather because of the strength of the 10-weight and a tippet that had the capability to derrick a six-pound rainbow trout far over one's head. Eventually, about 10 pounds of redfish tired and came to the boat. Henry gaffed the thing for the grill that night and I sat down from, well, too much sun.

"Get off your lame ass," Henry yelled between drags on a cigarette. He was smiling, so the situation appeared only mildly threatening for the present. "God. You fly all the way down here to sit and sweat. If you're going to sweat, at least work at it. I see three more up ahead."

Henry was smiling, and I caught a flash of light glinting off the gold tooth in the front of his mouth, a tooth that also had a piece of ivory shaped like a woman's breast embedded in it.

"Oh, what the hell," I thought as I stood up, slightly dizzy. This was certainly better than dealing with all those crazed, collect phone calls from my ex-wife (only number two so far—flyfishers and writers, especially those that practice both of these arcane forms of self abuse, rarely have much luck at sustaining a marginally sane, let alone happy domestic life, and I was no exception).

Henry was one of those people who liked to fish, a lot. He lived for the chase, the hunt, the sight of a wild fish moving in on a fly in the almost invisible liquid stillness of shallow water. When a bonefish, tarpon, or even the lowly (at least to some) redfish would move in on a pattern with deadly certainty, Henry's dark eyes would widen until the irises were mere dots surrounded by an oblong sea of white, faintly tinged with a discernible shading of red, a condition most likely the result of the previous night's consumption of booze at various bars scattered about the islands.

He had never missed a day on the water with a client and had told me as much on countless occasions. He liked to drink a lot in the evenings and, frequently, well into the night. Many of us are like that and live our lives with this often desperate awareness.

Henry never had much money. What he earned disappeared easily, with a certain *sui generis*. He maintained his boat, bar bills, and a little shack on an almost as small point of an obscure island. Henry lived here with the hordes of biting bugs, a few lizards, passing birds bound for somewhere else, and an aging hound of indeterminate lineage. There were times at bars when I'd watched him pay $20 for a two-dollar drink. But he was usually drunk by then and never noticed the difference.

"Who cares?" he said one morning when I mentioned this. He shrugged his shoulders with an expression on his face that said more than I needed to hear, then turned his attentions to starting the motor as I undid the lines that held the skiff to a gray, crumbling dock covered in splotches of off-white gull shit. Henry would never be rich; he drank too much and was without ambition or goals. He could care less about this, though he cared a good deal for the fish he constantly chased and for their diminishing habitat that was rapidly shrinking at the hands of developers. To say that Henry disliked this "rapacious horde," (his words) was a mild understatement. He'd spent a number of nights in jail for pulling up survey stakes and tearing down signs, and more often than not, he was drunk during these projects. For the most part, the local police used to look the other way. But as the Almighty *turista* dollar began to gain clout (buying up public officials and so forth), Henry's behavior moved through an obvious and regrettable progression from local character to nuisance to public menace.

I knew that his days were numbered out here, and he did, too. A local cop told me that Henry was "more than a pain in the ass," and that before long, he was going to wind up in the state prison for an extended stint of downtime. This would kill Henry, so I asked him why he didn't clean up his act some.

"Screw 'em. The bastards don't give a damn about all this." His arm moved across the horizon taking in the calm blue of the Gulf, the miles of white beaches, and the rich green of island growth. "When it's gone, I'm gone in a way. The bastards will have killed me and others like me for a quick fix. Bastards!"

Henry was well read, including the esoteric and painful likes of Joyce's *Finnegan's Wake*, Virginia Woolf's *To The Lighthouse*, and John Fante's *Bunker Hill* trilogy. But his favorite was Carl Hiaasen and his book, *Tourist Season*. The novel depicts the machinations of a Florida native who has had it with the ruthless modifications of a country he loves and the indiscriminate, uncaring behavior of the out-of-state yahoos descending from points north. One of the victims in the book is a Shriner. Another is the head of the Chamber of Commerce found suffocated with a rubber alligator shoved down his throat. Hiaasen, Henry, and I had a lot in common, it seemed.

Henry knew the book almost by heart and would often spout passages from memory while he poled languidly across the smooth flats.

"Off the bow, at the horizon, the sun seeped into a violet sky," I heard my friend's voice say, low but powerful in its passion. Somewhere out on Biscayne Bay, a flat red barge emitted three long whoops of warning, the most dolorous sound that Brian Keyes had ever heard. He clung to the wheel and waited.

"Fly!" he whispered. "Please fly away."

The lack of sound, not the silence, the absolute absence of anything when Henry was on one of these runs was hypnotic, terrifying, and exciting as hell: the edge many of us like to court with often deadly abandon. Everything was still, cold-cocked into mute submission. The fish were invisible. The water was like a pane of too clear glass made on another planet, and Henry staring off to God knows where, watching over a world he knew in his heart was not dying, but already dead.

If you haven't ever been where he could take you, a lot of this will seem crazy or plain foolish. "I don't care," as he says, "None of this matters anyway. It's all a cheap con." But when I am out there alone on the water with Henry, I know the awful truth of what he is saying. That all of the good stuff is dying or dead and that those of us who love wild places are out in them for only one reason—to say a lonely, last good-bye.

I'd met Henry some years back when he was augmenting his guiding income with a number of odd jobs. My parents lived on the southwestern shore of Gasparilla Island off of Boca Grande. Henry was a handyman who would fix the always-leaking roof or boards that were always rotting in the humid salt air. Since that time we'd become good friends, and I would stay at his place and fish the days away and burn down the nights. Henry showed me his prime spots and never thought of charging me a dime, except for some rum and maybe a steak or two. He liked to drink and smoke Camels—a pair of bad habits we had in common. Our conversations ranged from the bar fights he'd been in and the diminishing state of the economy as it applied to those like himself. But more importantly, he drove me nuts with stories of large tarpon coming into shore in late spring, of bonefish cruising the flats farther south, of redfish, sea trout, grouper, rays, battalions of shrimp on mating marches. These tales were marked by references to obscure bars hiding back in cypress-choked inlets, of drug runners and wild, rough, exotic women who could and did drink and dance all night in these places bubbling over with danger, adventure, and magic.

I never found out how old Henry was. Like I said earlier, for all I know, when I first saw him he could have been a weathered 35 or a tough 60. That was 10 or so years ago, and he looked the same, however, the years had revealed a growing sadness, a sense that his life was at least filled with irony and hard luck. He freely admitted that the bad times were his own "goddamned doing." Whether this was entirely true or not,

Henry never blamed anyone but himself. He even seemed to take a perverse pride in his varied misfortunes. In a society bent on pointing fingers, I found this refreshing in a harsh sort of way. He'd had little luck with women, but then who has. And his marriages (there had been four so far) and numerous affairs all had similar, dismal endings. But according to Henry, they contained more than enough elements of conflict, joy, and madness to fuel a dozen novels. I did not have the opportunity to meet his first, second, or fourth wife, but I did make the acquaintance of his third.

Barsey (an appropriate name, all things considered) was close to six feet tall with red hair that the sun had blasted the color of bright rubies. She had lavender eyes and a suntanned body whose wonderful dimensions could make a grown man cry deep down inside.

I met Barsey at the Pink Elephant one evening while having a few drinks to cool off from the heat. She recognized me from some pictures Henry had taken of one of our forays the year before. This big woman just walked over, sat on a stool next to me, and said in a smoky voice, "Hello, John."

I looked around, foolishly, to see who she was speaking to, but there was no one else near us. It had to be me, and all I could think was "Jesus!" She stared at me with a slight but knowing smile that said, "Are you getting a bit uncomfortable there, fella?" which I was.

"I used to be Henry's wife. His third, you know. I've seen pictures of you at his place and read a little of your books." She lit a Camel, sipped her drink, and ordered another in a motion as smooth as Brooks Robinson turning a 5-4-3 double play. I still couldn't think of a damn thing to say to her, and she laughed a little into her drink. I had to come up with something, anything. But I was dead on the water, befuddled as it were.

"For a writer you don't talk much, do you?" A cloud of mangled cigarette smoke coursed over my hands and swirled around the damp coolness of my drink, which was sweating almost as much as I was. "Henry said you two were heading out to the groves tomorrow. He hardly ever takes anyone there. It's his hideout. I call it his playpen when I want to piss him off. I expect him in for a belt in awhile."

"So do I." I was stunned at this spontaneous eloquence. "We've been known to have a few here on occasion."

"That's what I've heard. You look like a drinker," she said and another zephyr of smoke drifted across the rough surface of the badly scarred mahogany bar. "The few writers I've met all had the look, ya' know? Kind of a private gaze all their own. Actually, if you don't know the guy, it's a pain in the ass to be around, no offense intended."

"No offense taken. How the hell did you meet Henry, anyway?"

"In that run down old Episcopal church over by the Inn. There was a wedding. I knew the groom, and Henry, not surprisingly, knew the wife. We bumped into each other over drinks at the reception out back. From there we ended up at his place and things went way off from there. We were married a week later."

"You waited that long?"

I ordered us another round, and she blew more smoke toward the slowly turning overhead fan.

"A wise ass, too," she said, "but I'd heard that from Henry. Yah. It was a quickie. Six months of fun and connubial bliss as they say. Then the damn water and the goddamned fish started calling. That was it in less than a month. I never saw him. Always on the water or in the bars or pulling up survey stakes. I couldn't take it and moved out. We were divorced a little while later. Another quickie. Neither of us had shit for money or cars or furniture. Nothing to fight over, really. Kind of a loss, but fun all the same."

Henry was that type of guy. The best of intentions, but long-term commitments were a foreign concept. I knew about the hold that the water, the fish, and the booze could exert on a person. Hell, I drank too much, too often, was probably an alcoholic. And to make things worse, I didn't really give a damn. A lot of us were like that. Henry being one of the most accomplished at throwing away the good things that looked more like work to many of us. I imagined that someday he would receive a lifetime achievement award for irresponsible behavior. I'd already been nominated several times, but the judging committee felt that my body of work was incomplete at this stage. Give me time, boys. Give me time.

Barsey turned and edged closer. A subtle, musky, citrus smell filled the air between us.

"Royal Lime," she said. "It's for men. But I like it, so screw 'em," Her drink took a serious hit; the ice chimed musically in her glass.

"How'd you know?" I asked.

"Your nose twitched like a twisted rabbit. Finish your drink. It's my turn."

We passed several hours drinking at an increasingly leisurely pace, talking about Henry, the rape of Florida, writers, and favorite books. She loved Exley's *Pages from a Cold Island*. But he's dead and when I mentioned this, Barsey said, "So what? We're all dead in a way. Some more than others."

In the course of our verbal meanderings, I learned that she had earned her master's in biology up in Tallahassee years ago, worked for some firm in Orlando, been fired because she "didn't play well with others," and now made a few bucks selling prints of her photographs of the Gulf and its residents at galleries around the area. Money was not an issue with her as long as there was enough for the monthly bills and a few drinks. The rest took care of itself.

I was familiar with the concept.

The bar was pretty much empty around midnight, but the bartender, Fred, was in no hurry and started bringing us drinks without our asking or paying.

Barsey had returned to Henry convinced that his increasing vehemence regarding the destruction of the environment and his growing agitation with developers, tourists, and the government was going to finish him off long before the "damn booze."

"Sure he cares, but he's using this as an excuse to blow off his anger at the whole damn trip," she said while lighting another Camel. "Some of you guys just can't hack the bullshit. You take it all so personally. Give it up, for Jesus."

It was at this cheery juncture that Henry blew through the screen door, which slammed against the inside wall then weakly swung shut.

"There you are, Johnny, and drinking with my wife, you bastard." Henry was lit but in obvious good spirits. Eyes glowing. Face flushed. Full tilt.

"Ex-wife, dear. And after living with you, I sure as hell want nothing to do with a derelict writer, especially if he's a friend of yours. Jesus, God, you two are a pair. How you manage to avoid drowning in that lame boat of yours or wrecking that truck, I'll never know. God shines on lunatics."

Barsey pushed away from the bar and set sail for the jukebox behind us. I could hear quarters being shoved down the slot and then Bob Seger and the Silver Bullet Band started in on The Fire Inside. Good stuff. Spinning on one heel, Barsey strolled with understated confidence back to the bar. If she was drunk, which I knew I was, she didn't show it. The woman could hold her booze. "Another one boys? Fred, make these triples. Time to winnow the chaff from the wheat. Shouldn't take long with these two clowns." All of this was said behind a friendly but wicked grin you had to see to appreciate.

"Ready to go fishing tomorrow, Johnny? Hell, you can't cast for shit and won't catch anything, but what the hell. The groves are sweet."

Henry polished off the triple in one upright slash, walked out through the traumatized screen door, and yelled behind him, "See you at five."

Barsey and I closed the place talking a lot about nothing, and then she offered to drive me home.

Home turned out to be her place and some drinks and a little more, I think.

It was barely daybreak and I thought the world was coming to an end, that we'd been nuked. Perhaps Clinton and the boys had finally lost it up in D.C.

BANG. BANG. BANG. BANG. BANG.

"Henry, cool it. I'll get him moving." Barsey jabbed me, hard, in the ribs.

I fell off the bed and onto the floor, found my jeans and shirt, and dressed with less than graceful haste.

"Henry, how'd you know I'd be here?"

"Go figure," and he grabbed a pair of Busch from the refrigerator, tossing one to me as I entered the kitchen that exploded in icy foam when I popped the lid. I love a breakfast beer or two or three, and today was already off the books. I'd seen enough of these suckers ride down on me with the sun rise to know that tomorrow would be a painful experience. Oh well, you can't dance, as they say.

"Let the bastard get any sleep, Bars?" Henry laughed loudly around slurps of beer. "Come on Johnny. We've got beer, rum, food, a full tank of gas, and a clean windshield. As good a day to die as any. Sun's almost up."

Barsey said good-bye with her eyes and added that she'd see us at the tavern tonight if we managed to hang on to "our ragged asses."

"Kill something for me," she yelled from the porch as we struck off in a cloud of dust and exhaust that hung on the calm, damp morning air.

I was still a bit out of it from the night before, but felt good. A little maintenance with the beer and I might make it to the tavern tonight. Bela Fleck was on the tape player. The day promised sun and heat, and Henry looked happy and at ease. I decided to forego the bonefishing clothes and burn a bit today, and in minutes we were racing over the smooth water headed south.

Henry's Whaler had a 175 and a smaller motor for close-in work. We flew over the surface on plane, the wind rushed across my face like a woman's breath. I had no idea where we were going, but talk about being alive.

We cut into a channel lined with cypress and other leafy plants I couldn't identify. Then we shifted to the smaller engine as the course narrowed, and soon we were moving under a dense canopy that turned the early-morning light green-gold.

Birds blew up through the growth as we rounded each bend—egrets and others that I again could not identify. The air smelled sweet and rich with an abundance of life. Primal. Quiet, even with the sound of the motor pushing us ever deeper into the wilderness. It was hard to believe that highways, high-rises, mile after mile of hideous malls, and malignant cities were around somewhere not too far away.

After about 20 minutes we eased under some low-flying limbs and broke out into a small lagoon. Here the water was deep and clear, and it was dead quiet when Henry cut the motor.

"Cast that dinky-shit 8-weight of yours tight to the roots," commanded Henry. "There's baby tarpon in here. Maybe a snook or two." Then he rigged his own battered rod, also an 8-weight, which wore an old Pflueger with nicked-up line and a large white and red streamer tied to the end. Pushing right into the plants, we worked out about 60 feet of line. The patterns landed with a soft "plop," and we let the streamers sink a bit before making quick, stripping retrieves.

On the second cast, the water exploded and a silver rocket (a friend of Seger's?) blasted into the air and then raced for cover. Henry yanked the fish back to safe holdings and let it have its way with him, and then my rod was almost jerked from my hands and another silver missile made a raucous appearance. Both of us watched with lunatic smiles as our tarpon roared around the pond. Both reels sang with ratchety enthusiasm as the fish pulled well into our backings.

Henry soon brought his to boat—a 12-pounder—released it, and stood watching me make a spectacle of myself. The fish zigged and zagged about 40 feet out, often breaking the water and shaking its head, the spray sparkling like affordable diamonds in the hard light. Eventually the tarpon (another 12-pounder) gave up and I brought him in. Henry twisted the hook free with a pair of zircon pliers and turned it loose. It vanished in a metallic "whoosh." Then all was silence again.

A Busch came winging my way, bouncing off my chest and falling to the platform. Another liquid explosion and the beer tasted cold and good as it bubbled into my gut.

"What do you think of the groves now, you silly bastard?" The grin on Henry's face is what I fish for. This is what the game is all about. Good friends. Good fish. Good country. I was home. "I found this about ten years ago lost one night. Stayed 'til dawn and couldn't believe the water when the sun came up. Six casts, six tarpon. Not big, but fun, and nobody's here to bug me."

"The place has a certain intrinsic charm to it," I offered.

"Any more of that sissy crap and I'll keep the beer to myself. Let's try up there where that little flow slides in."

We both launched casts to either side of the inlet where tarpon tagged the flies immediately. Mine quickly leaped beneath some cypress and snapped off, breaking a few limbs as it did so. Henry pulled his into the open, playing the fish with discreet skill and determination before releasing it, a little fish of, maybe, 15 pounds. And the day went pretty much like that.

We worked the lagoon and a couple of others farther in and caught tarpon to 18 pounds and one confused snook. The place was special. A million miles from anywhere. Time vanished and everything was so focussed it was like being on another planet, doing a strange drug, unreal. I asked Henry why the fish were here at this time of the year. Wasn't it the off-season?

"They're always here," he stated matter of factly. "Don't believe all that crap you read in the magazines. Those fools don't have a clue. They say the fish aren't here now. What the hell do you think we've been catching all damn day?"

The air was hot and the beer was making me drowsy, in a pleasant sort of way.

"Had enough?," asked Henry.

"Never enough, but plenty for today. What time is it?"

"About four and we've got a couple of hours in. Let's go and cleanup, have a quick lie down, and then wander off to find Bars.

After a few pregame, warm-up rum and Cokes, we strolled down to the tavern, a ramshackle, wood building leaning longingly towards the water on a side channel off the Gulf.

Zeke's, or Zek's if you went by the pink neon sign glowing over the entrance in the fading light, had wooden flooring that tilted in angles heading off in all directions. It was a place settling into the ground, moving to its own rhythms. Most of the stools in front of the long wooden bar were occupied by locals, but we found a pair of empties at the far end. We ordered drinks and munched on big, homemade pretzels crusted with chunks of salt.

The sound of conversation filled the room, just enough to make the atmosphere comfortable, not empty or obnoxious. A huge tarpon hung above the long, cloudy mirror over a row of booze bottles. Duke Ellington and "It Ain't Necessarily So" was playing on a stereo, which sat next to an antique cash register. No Jimmy Buffett? No "Cheeseburger in Paradise"? And this was Florida? Thank God. I'd only been here once before. Briefly, to pick up a six-pack, but even during that short stop I knew immediately that Zeke's was my kind of place. The well-healed, monied snowbirds from up north had been waging a constant campaign to close the bar; bad for the island's image or something equally inane.

"You know, I've seen big tarpon where we were today. Over a hundred pounds. Near dark on a full moon," said Henry. "I've only jumped one and he broke me off. They seem to have other things on their minds, but it sure would be fun to try and land one in that small water in the dark. Need at least a 10-weight and one hell of a wire leader, but it could be done."

"When's the next full moon?"

"In six days," he said while scanning the bar and nodding "Hello" to almost everybody. "You going to be here that long?"

"I am now. Stuff like that intrigues me. Where's Barsey?"

"She'll be in soon enough. Usually by 10."

At the hour she wandered up to us, appearing seemingly out of nowhere. She was barefoot and wearing cutoffs and a Fred Imus T-shirt adorned with a turquoise buffalo. She smelled of Royal Lime.

"I see you two slap-happy bastards got away with another one," and she reached for a drink that also appeared out of thin air. "How'd you do? You kill one of those overgrown mackerel for me?"

"I don't hurt those fish," Henry said with the merest hint of edge to his voice.

"Whatever will you do, dear, when they develop your playpen?" she said, and the wicked grin surfaced again.

"Anyone who screws with that water will pay, big time." The word "playpen" did piss Henry off. "The bastards can leave me something. Christ, they've got that abortion Disney World. Enough's enough," and he drained his drink as three more arrived unannounced. Henry's face glowed red, even beneath the dark tan. "Goddamnit, Bars. Don't get me started here."

She backed off and we talked, again about not much of anything, until well past midnight, and when I returned from an excursion to the men's room, Henry was gone.

"Where'd he go?"

"You know Henry. Here today...," Barsey said around a cigarette. "Looks like it's just you and me again. God help us all." She was right about that, too, but what with the rum and Cokes and the intoxicating ambiance of Zeke's, I figured, what the hell?

"Who the heck is Zeke, anyway?"

"An old friend of Henry's. Died of bone cancer or some thing like that years ago. No one knows what caused it, but Henry's convinced it's from chemicals from the plants up north that moved down here in the groundwater. Zeke was a good guy." Her expression softened, just a touch, for the first time since I'd known her.

"That's what pushed Henry over the edge on this environmental stuff. That and the dying fish out there." She swung a long arm out toward the Gulf. The red, green, and blue-white lamps of cargo ships flickered on the water. Deep-throated horns boomed in the distance. The ships were talking to each other with light and sound. "The water is his life. They're killing him with all their mad schemes." And I could see that, despite her giving Henry grief, Barsey was a kindred soul. Another of the lost ones who knew it was all over, but knew she didn't have to like it. She was fighting, in her own way, the obscenity that Florida is becoming. These two were good people. I wish there were a whole lot more of them, and that made me sad all the way down to my stomach, so I ordered us one of her famous triples. We drank in silence. The hands on the clock closed in on two.

We stayed for another drink or three past closing time, a nebulous concept that was not strictly enforced, then she drove me home again to her place. She put on some old Ornette Coleman, and we passed the time enjoying each other's company, talking very little.

Around 4 a.m. she took my hand and led me to the bedroom where she made love to me in a way that seemed to say I wasn't quite as bad as I often gave myself credit for. A good woman who'd learned how to make the best out of a tough life. We fell asleep in each other's arms.

The phone started ringing, loudly, about six. My head hurt, some.

Barsey picked up the receiver. "Yes? How bad? I'll be right down."

God. What now? I thought. Does anybody sleep past sunrise around here?

"Henry's in jail and beat up. Drove a D-9 into a canal and they caught him at it. One of them is in the hospital in bad shape," she said. "Damn. I knew this would happen. Get dressed."

We piled into her rusting Jag, both of us looking like escapees from a rain delayed, extra-inning night game in Cleveland. The jail was a mile away in a newer, cement block building colored tan, the paint already peeling away in large strips. The cops knew Barsey and definitely knew Henry. We were escorted to his cell. He was alone and lying on his back. You could see the bruises around his puffed-up eyes and along his arms. His shirt was torn and bloody, as were his chinos. He looked a mess.

"Henry. Henry!"

"Bars. Johnny. I guess I messed up on this one." Henry sat up slowly with a groan. "They were laying for me and I was too smashed to move fast enough. Got one of them good, though. What's the bail, girl?"

"More money than we've got, buddy. I'll see what I can do when the place wakes up. My guess is you're here for awhile." Barsey tossed a pack of smokes through the bars. "I think you earned six months on this one, Henry, damnit."

"Johnny, I guess the moonlight ride is off for this year. Bars will entertain you, maybe even drive you to the airport next week." He stubbed out his cigarette on the sweating wall.

We all talked some more, then Barsey and I left. The day was fruitless as for raising money. The bail was too steep and everyone wanted Henry to stay put, to pay his dues, the bastards.

Barsey and I killed off the week reading, lying in the sun, talking, drinking, and screwing. I visited my friend one last time prior to leaving for Bradenton and the flight home. Barsey waited outside. Henry was himself as usual, but six months in the county jail was a long ride. I couldn't do it. I hoped he'd survive. There wasn't much to say and we both knew it.

Just before heading out, I asked if there was anything I could do for him.

"Just get your ass back down here next year, Johnny."

T · W · O

Dancing on the Bitterroot

MARCH IS A FINE TIME OF THE YEAR IN MONTANA. Winter is almost dead. Most of the snow has melted and what remains is old and gray and crusty. Sure, there are still storms that whistle down from Canada, but then again, there are those days in the 60s and even 70s, which are filled with warm breezes and fluffy clouds motoring across the sky. Some of the migrating birds are back—robins, ducks, and flocks of geese honking their way overhead in the darkness late at night. The land is coming back to life and so, too, are fly-fishers. Admittedly, we're a sad lot; sacrificing jobs, marriages, and social responsibility in mad pursuit of our arcane passion. By the end of February we'd tied enough flies to outfit half of Pierre, South Dakota (not as hard is it may first seem). Rods, lines, and reels have been cleaned, greased, oiled, and polished. All of our gear has been organized to a state of high neuroticism, though this order will rapidly degenerate into random chaos as the fishing moves into high gear.

Guides are no exception when it comes to this ritualized mayhem. Broke or almost so, behind on payments that include a battered pickup, the house (if it hasn't already been foreclosed upon), bar bills, and the like, these intrepid and slightly off-key individuals can't wait to hit the water. Avon rafts are shipshape—all leaks patched, Carlisle oars repaired and ropes replaced. Springtime in the Rockies.

For me, this delightful process is no more evident than down on the Bitterroot where several of my friends make their living from the river, the trout, and those who spend good money for the privilege of a professional guide's knowledge, expertise, and company. The Bitterroot is a beautiful stream filled with rainbows, browns, westslope cutthroat, brook, and bull trout. The river glides between the Sapphire Mountains on the east and the rugged Selway-Bitterroots to the west, twisting and bending through a wide, agrarian valley. Huge cottonwoods tower above water that bubbles and churns over rock and a gravel streambed of colorful stone. Undercut banks, deep holes, dark runs, swirling pools, and dense log-jams provide prime habitat for trout that occasionally exceed 20 inches: wallhangers, as they say—powerful, brightly colored, muscular fish that love a good dry fly or a dredged nymph or a twitching streamer. At times they are even forgiving of a sloppy presentation or a poor mend. This is sweet water, as good as it gets, anywhere. Maybe that's why there are a number of very talented guides hanging out in places like Missoula, Stevensville, Hamilton, and Darby.

My favorite is Bob Dernier, a long-time friend and a 1969 (69er as he puts it) high school graduate who lives in the mountains west of the river and south of Stevensville. Bob has been working the Bitterroot for many years and knows the water as well as anyone. We first met on the Smith River one blustery day in May, a float that, incidentally, featured a few browns coaxed from chocolate-colored water that rose steadily with the melting snow and incessant rain and sleet. Five days together along with six others in three more rafts. Slow fishing but a good time in great country. Excellent food, a bit to drink around a nightly fire, and plenty of BS. My kind of trip.

Since that time, Bob and I have managed to fish the Bitterroot at least once a year, usually in March when a large, gray, and relatively unknown stonefly called the *skwala* begins to hatch.

Big trout, normally rainbows and browns, key in on the ungainly bug. It's their first real meal since the previous fall: an insectivorous banquet of sorts. Especially when the sun is shining, a #8 tie looking something like an elk hair or a fashion-conscious hopper turns the trick when cast near rocky, cobbled shorelines around mid-afternoon. Bob is a superb caster and can read water with the best of them, but he never gives me too much grief when I miss a "bucket" or an inside seam or miss a take or break off a good trout. He figures, what the hell, we're out here to have fun, the rest is gravy. When I do bring a large fish to net he is as excited as I am, always shouting, "Good job. Nice fish, John. Way to go." We admire the husky brown or crimson-striped rainbow briefly as it holds in the water next to the raft prior to release. Then we laugh a bit and sip a beer, and I'll often smoke a Camel while Bob wades out to work the far bank, casting with tight loops, midair mends, and gentle drifts that more often than not turn a fish. We spend long, peaceful afternoons this way. Drifting, taking trout, stopping along the way to work over some decent water, talking about the Chicago Bulls, the government, the environment (always the environment), music, and friends we have in common. I can't think of a better way to kill off a day or a better man to do it with.

"What do you think about the Bulls getting Rodman?" he'll ask over his shoulder in a deep voice filled with intensity, dark eyes flashing with mad delight. I'm sitting in the back. Less scrutiny and more room to move. God only knows what I do back there when no one is looking. "He can board with the best of them, but he's a real head case. Think Jackson can keep him and Jordan and Pippen happy all year? What a zoo that will be."

I agree and we go on for long minutes about the team and the rest of the NBA. We're both inveterate Chicago sports fans. The real kind. We grew up with the disease. The Cubs, Bears, Blackhawks, Bulls. If they play in Chicago (with the possible exception of the White Sox), we know their all too often sad histories and our woeful legacies. But who's complaining; we wouldn't have things any other way.

Today we start around one p.m. and the day is perfect. Not much wind, temperature in the 50s and a high overcast with the sun shining through like a dim bulb. The water is low and clear, the air still marked with the scent of last fall and the smell of slowly decaying leaves blended nicely with the rich, fertile fragrance of the river. A few Baetis and a random skwala or two buzzed in the air. Can the *Ameletus* and green drakes be far behind?

Bob pulls the raft carefully into the water, and I climb aboard with a grace and dignity that manages to spare the rod. He laughs, pulls us into the current, and pushes off, rowing strongly to a small island that holds a nice run. I strip out line and cast quartering slightly ahead, throwing a small upstream mend in the line. The fly bobs within inches of the dead grass that overhangs the water and appears clear-copper as it dances over the bottom. Ten feet of drift and a pair of lips surface and deliberately suck in my bug. I set the hook and a brown rolls immediately, shaking its head at the same time. Bob rows to calm water and I play the fish as it bulldogs in the current before coming to us on its side. Sixteen inches, red-spotted with a golden yellow belly. A nice way to start a new year. One cast. One good fish.

"Better than last year, John," Bob comments in reference to our maiden voyage 12 months ago, one that featured gale-force winds, temperatures around freezing, rain, sleet, and two trout. We survived, but we were cold, wet, and miserable. Today was going to be different. That was obvious. I looked behind me at Trapper Peak, a jagged piece of rock that rose thousands of feet above the valley floor. Covered in many feet of snow that flickered in the sunlight as purple clouds swirled around its summit. Nasty up that high, but pleasant down in the shelter of the stream course. I shed my wax-cotton coat and roll up the sleeves on my sweater. Christ! What a day. Good-bye winter.

We shove off again and Bob pulls us over to the other side, a long, brushy, root-choked run that always holds nice browns, maybe 20 inches on a fortuitous day. The water runs swift and hard, looking to all the world like a fishless location, at least to neo-phytes, yupsters, and assorted other flotsam polluting our rivers. But all along the bank there are places of calm, shelter, watery quietude that the fish love. Throw a bug tight, turn a dragless drift, and the trout will move like jets with afterburners kicked in, ham-mering the skwala and then pulling hard for cover.

Bob worked back against the current so that we moved down the bank slightly slower than the current about 25 feet out. I cast next to shore, the fly bouncing off a rock and drift-ing inches away, then a brown flashed beneath and hammered the offering, setting the hook on its own. She thrashed the sur-face and tried to gain the sanctity of the undercut bank but was unsuccessful as we moved across stream. A few strong runs downstream and then a tired submissive ride to the raft. Eighteen inches this time. Fat and full of color, with only a sprinkling of blood-red spots along its flanks. We watched as the brown swam away from us, held in shallow water while regaining its equilibrium, then streaking off into the depths. This was easy, uncommonly so for a change.

"Let's pull over along that gravel bar down there and work the pool and riffle," Bob suggested. The float was only a few miles to put in and downstream to takeout at our friend Vic Davalio's lodge, a rambling, log structure perched on a bank above the river. One of the nicest places to fish and just hang out that I've ever run across. This short distance to cover afforded us plenty of opportunities and time to stop and seriously work over prime water along the way and still be at the lodge in time for a cocktail or two and a leisurely dinner followed by some sports on TV. A rough life down here on the Bitterroot.

Bob walked well downriver and began casting upstream. I did the same starting from the beached raft. Within two casts both of us had fish on. Mine a nice rainbow of 16 or 17 inches, while Bob's looked to be a brown of larger dimensions. The rainbow leaped several times, smacking the water with its sil-very, wide sides. I don't think I've ever caught a trout in this river that wasn't in good shape. Excellent water quality, an abundance of invertebrate species in large numbers, and plenty of holding water all combined in synergistic fashion to create ideal conditions. I watched as Bob brought the brown to him, the fish splashing and resisting his efforts the whole way. We plied the water for another 30 minutes or so, taking fish at regular intervals. We could quit right now and I'd be satisfied, but some of the best water lay ahead.

We sat on the side of the raft chewing on corn chips, salsa, and elk sandwiches laced with onion and peppers (a Mexican delight here in western Montana) washed down with a little Milwaukee cerveza—Schlitz.

Bob looked around at the lay of the land, taking in the day and a pair of hawks soaring far above us. The air moved softly with a hint of the warmth to come in a few months. A few remaining yellow and brown aspen leaves lay scattered across the surface of the river, bouncing along the riffles, and swirling in the nebula-like foamy eddies below us. All along the far overgrown bank, we saw good-sized trout feeding on both Baetis and the random skwala. In another half-hour the hatch should have been up to speed with about a 45-minute window where the fishing could be outrageous. But so far, the fish that had taken our imitations were doing so out of familiarity. They knew the stoneflies were hatching on a daily basis and were beginning to key in to them.

But then, like a cloud passing in front of the sun, I saw my friend's face darken

"What's up, Bob?"

"Just thinking about when all the fucking jet boats and one-man rafts are going to start showing up on the river," Bob stated glumly. "The damn things. Seems like the more I float, the more of them I see. I tell the bastards, I'm going to stay ahead of you and if that means rowing over your water, tough shit. Most of the ones who use them can't kick hard enough to stay away from the banks. They put down all the damn trout. I think I'll carry an AK-47 to level the playing field," and Bob flashed a nasty smile. He may well have meant it, for all I knew. "Damn Davalio is thinking of putting a deck cannon on his raft. I can just see him launching one in front of a group of those things or sinking a jet boat. What a sight that would be. I can just see one of those idiots going down for the count."

Bob was referring to the increasing numbers of one man, raft-like contrivances that a growing field of manufacturers are hustling in fly shops and in the major fly fishing magazines. Used properly, they are perhaps only a minor nuisance, but most of the Bozos haven't a clue, running pell-mell down stream ruining the fishing for all of us. The marketing ploy runs something along the lines of "Hey, they're cheap. Every man can be captain of his own ship. Why pay someone when you can be your own guide." They're cheap alright, and most of them resemble constipated spiders with terminal cases of elephantiasis. Ugly things that do more harm than good.

As for jet boats and jet skis. Sink 'em all. They destroy the banks with their wakes. Traumatize the fish and destroy the aesthetics of a river. Their only redeeming value may lie as artificial habitat as they corrode into sweet oblivion at the bottom of a deep, dark pool. Where's my gun?

As for the owners of these noisome abortions, make them daytime talk show hosts or, at least, members of the audience. Let them amuse the simpering fools who watch the likes of Leeza and Geraldo, but keep them off the water, please.

"John, that's a bad look on your face," and we both laugh at our internal soapbox, righteous intensity. "Screw it for now. Let's head on down to those working fish. Their ripe for the taking." We shoved off into the current, bad thoughts temporarily stored away somewhere unnoticeable.

The browns that were delicately sipping Baetis with epicurean discrimination would require soft casts, drag-free floats and light tippets. I added a section of 5X to the piece of 4X that was a bit frazzled in the last few inches; no doubt from the chewing at the hands of the previous fish. I tied on a #18 blue-winged olive that Bob had created. A beautiful fly with a white tuft on top to aid in visibility. I worked out about 35 feet of line and tossed a reach cast to the bank. The chute floated to the surface and rode quietly down on a large brown. Had I timed the cast to match the trout's feeding pattern? Apparently so as the fish took the fly in a swirl. I set the hook by pulling slowly and steadily back. As soon as the brown felt the prick of the point all hell broke loose with the fish tearing apart the water and then trying to use the force of the current against its sides to pull free from this foreign hindrance to its freedom. The fight wasn't flashy, just determined, and my right arm was actually tiring from putting pressure on the slender tippet. Eventually, the trout broke off its hold in the current and came to net. A nice, fat colorful male just short of 20 inches. I held it by the tail while the oxygen-rich water flowed through its gills. Within seconds I felt its muscles quiver as the brown tried to pull free from my grasp. I relaxed my hold and the fish was gone in a flash, cutting a small vee in the shallow water and kicking up weak clouds of detritus as it pulsed its tail.

"You can live with that one, can't you John," Bob said with a sly grin and a wink.

"It'll have to do for know. Pass me a beer and that jar of jalapeños, Dernier." We drifted around a sharp curve in the river, where charcoal gray rock cliffs rose above us. Willows lined the bank and small aspen clung to the steep sides with precarious intensity. Clouds obscured the sun and a puff of breeze turned the day cool for a change. Then the cover rode off over the eastern horizon, the sun broke loose, the afternoon turned warm, and I could see skwalas on the surface, working their way up the cobbled bank downstream from us. Post time, I drained the beer and passed the peppers back to Bob. The river was narrow here, and we moved to the far shore, but the cast would be, at most, 25 feet out and several more downstream with the mend.

I pushed the line out and along the inside seam next to shore. The chute was easy to see, but then it was gone and I saw the flash of a brown with my fly in its mouth as it headed down to the benthic shelter along the river's bottom. At first the trout did not know it was hooked, but as soon as we moved below it and into shallow water I exerted a touch of pressure and the fish went straight up the water column and into the air, jumping twice and sparkling brown and coppery silver in the light. A long one into the backing, another leap, and another run and the brown tired. I got up and walked down to the fish, reeling in line as I went. Bob netted it, a fine fish of 20, maybe 21 inches. The barbless hook slid out easily and the trout was gone without our tender revivalistic ministrations.

"This is too damn easy, Bob. The hook sets itself and the goofy trout stay out in the open, and I haven't even clenched down on one yet. What am I doing wrong? I should have broken off a half-dozen by now." I was puzzled with this apparent spate of good fortune and prodigious angling skill. A rare combination in my experience.

"Maybe you're still straight, Holt. Have another beer."

"I'll pass for now. This is too nice to waste. Onward and upward," and away we went in search of more action. Dernier pulled his rod out of the case and rigged up. He began casting while holding in the middle of the river with the oars tucked beneath his armpits. Such coordination. I was in awe and said so.

"Kiss off, Holt," and the line whizzed quite close to my ear on his backcast. Bob had on a small Baetis imitation also. The pattern landed just above a nice bucket formed where a small rush of sideflow hit the main current. There was an area of relative calm in the middle of this watery structure with seams bringing food and oxygen in on both sides. A big fish hole. The fly crested a slight rise in the current then dropped down on the inside and a huge fish tagged the imitation, then raced downstream. Bob's reel made a lot of noise in protest to this obvious insult to its dignity, but it was to no avail. The brown snapped sideways in the current while charging full-speed ahead, and the tippet popped with an audible ping. The brown jumped three times in quick succession, its body forming a perfect arc as it leaped, flew, and then crashed back into the river.

"Jesus, that was a big, god-damn fish." Even the unflappable Dernier looked a bit shaken.

"I'd say at least two feet, Bob. I bet that's the same one you turned there last October, only I think the bastard put on some weight."

"I'll get it before the year's over." Bob was determined and I had little doubt about the outcome. That buck brown was history in a manner of speaking, as it was just a matter of time when Bob put his head to something.

The rest of the float was more of the same with the browns outnumbering the rainbows about three-to-one. The trout averaged around 16 inches, and toward the end of the float, on the last mile before Davalio's lodge, the skwalas disappeared and we switched to nymphs—hare's ears and Princes with a little weight but no strike indicators—hardcore.

Shorter casts of 15 to 20 feet and tight lines turned some nice fish including one brown that came close to 20 inches. Rounding a sharp twist in the Bitterroot and gliding beneath a thick stand of cottonwoods and Ponderosa pine, we spotted a group of turkeys "putting" and "purting" their ungainly way back into the trees. Several whitetails raised their flags and bounded out of sight. Then, the lodge came into view on our left and we were finished for the day. A couple of dozen fish, decent weather, marginal conversation—who could ask for more. Davalio spied us from a window in the main room of the lodge and ambled down to the take out.

"How'd you guys do?" he asked as he helped unload our gear. "Beautiful day to be fishing. The river set up perfectly."

"Holt missed every damn fish we saw, except for those he broke off. You'd think he was trying to hook tarpon," Dernier said as he placed the oars on shore. "Geez, you'd think I'd learn by now not to waste my time with the guy. Damn near took my ear off twice with one of those awful buggers he ties with fuse wire. Hit a duck with one of those things and it dies. Right there in midair. I'm taking your camcorder next time. Nobody would believe the crap he pulls on the river. It's unbelievable. Tragic."

"Thanks Dernier. Forget your tip. I'd saved a six pack of warm Pabst as a reward for all your hard work, but you kissed that off."

Dernier walked up to get his truck, so we didn't have to run the shuttle. Davalio rode up to the put-in with a friend while we were floating and brought the rig back down. Then went to work in the bunkhouse, which doubled as his living quarters as well as an office where he labored hard at screwing up high-paying clients' tax returns. Several were reportedly on death row or had committed suicide rather than face an audit with Davalio at their sides. Rumor, though extremely vague in nature, did have it that Davalio had actually saved one client over $11 back in 1990, but this was unconfirmed and subject to legitimate skepticism. Fortunately, I didn't make enough money to require my friend's services.

"I started the fire and put a turkey on the coals. Should be ready in an hour or so. And I opened a few bottles of a California Cab I picked up when I was back in the land of LA," said Davalio with a grin that was accentuated by a thick black mustache. "The Bulls and Cleveland are on in a few minutes."

We motored to the lodge, quickly stored our gear, and poured some wine. Things were awfully damn tough at Davalio's place. My home away from home on the road. Door #3 was mine and I'd surely sleep like the dead.

There are a lot of nice rivers and valleys in Montana, and that's why I live here. But the Bitterroot is special. That's all there is to it. The drainage is just flat out special—good country, water, and people and less than four hours from my home up north in the Flathead. God, life was tough out here. You'll never see this kid hanging around the mean streets of Beloit, Wisconsin, again. No way. No how. What a nightmare that would be.

Davalio already had the playoffs on the tube but it was a few minutes to tipoff, so we all wandered out to the front deck to check on the progress of the bird, which happened to be doing quite nicely on the massive stone grill that sported a giant elk rack mounted in cement on the crown of the structure. A rectangular opening in the middle of the thing perfectly framed Trapper Peak rumbling skyward in the western distance. Davalio had a certain flair and knew how to do things right, tax returns excepted (just kidding, actually he was accomplished at what he did for a living and could hold his own with the boys from the IRS).

He had a special way of roasting the turkey, too, setting the bird in an aluminum pan surrounded by 21 briquettes on each side to which 16 more were added, again on each side as the cooking progressed. He claimed he learned the trick from a chef he knew in California. Perhaps, but the process turned out the best, juiciest turkey I'd ever eaten. Along with a tossed salad, an Idaho baker, and some more of his top-shelf wines, dining was an event to look forward to while meandering down river.

The meal was ready at the end of the first quarter—Bulls 33, Cavs 28—as we devoured the food, the plump turkey savagely reduced to a ragged, bare-bones carcass. The sight of three large, grown men eating with such enthusiasm, what with juice dripping down our chins, sour cream clinging to our finger tips, and bottles of wine dying ugly deaths, would surely appear horrifying and grotesque to an innocent bystander.

We staggered over to couches and easy chairs in front of the game and a roaring fire. Talk of fishing mingled with comments on the game. Jordan was out of shape, the trout weren't. Jackson had to be nuts to try and cope with Pippen's ego. The skwalas were starting to come on strong and so forth. Game over. Bulls winning 118-112. Dernier headed home promising that he'd meet us before noon, and I passed through door #3 crashing into bed and out of consciousness, lost in the ozone again.

I woke with the day's first light to the sound of honking geese winging their way to breakfast. Walking along the deck to the main room the air felt icy. Thick frost covered the grass, turning it silver and gray. I fired up some water to pour over some double roast Italian coffee I'd brought down from Whitefish. Good and strong with a touch of sugar. Three cups and I was ready to start calling my editors in New York and start demanding higher rates for my work and money up front to boot. I settled, instead for building a warm fire, making another pot of coffee, munching on bagels, and reading old issues of *Gray's Sporting Journal*: decadence honed to a fine art.

Several deer were browsing beneath the Ponderosa. Black-capped chickadees, Juncos, and creepers flitted around the bird feeders. The sky was turning from deep blue to robin's-egg blue, and an orange glow was building over the hills on the far side of the river, which provided nice background music as it tumbled over rocks and gravel. Not a cloud in the sky. The skwalas would be out big time and the fish would throw blue-sky caution to the wind to feed on the succulent bugs. It was going to be a tough day, but we'd survive. Davalio was busting loose from work for the afternoon to lend his own special brand of piscatorial expertise to the expedition.

I heard the screen door to the kitchen open and then slam shut.

"Holt. You're up. I thought you might die in your sleep. After cleaning up I walked down to the wood pile. It sounded like you'd swallowed your tongue. What a racket." Davalio broke into a staccato laughter that came from deep inside. A nice sound. "You even made coffee. Divorce seems to suit you." (Year two of living alone was proving to be much better than year one. There was even a woman or two in the offing back home. Free at last. Free at last.)

"The river looks super today," he said, looking out the window at the Bitterroot as it rushed against a large boulder resting in the middle of the current and steam from the coffee swirling around his face. "What time did Dernier say he'd be here?"

"A little before noon."

"I'll be ready. I've got to get back to my returns. Crunch time approaches."

"Sandwiches, chips, and salsa okay for lunch?"

"Suits me. There's some roast ducks left in the frig and Louise (the lodge's cook for visiting dignitaries) made some garlic mayonnaise. It's in a brown crock on the door."

I finished off the coffee and another bagel before plunging into the sandwich making. Two large ones apiece on rye bread with sliced Bermuda onion, the duck, mayo, a touch of coarse mustard, and some lettuce. Two bags of corn chips, a jar of salsa, and some Snickers bars. It's amazing the attention food receives when outdoor activities are on tap. At home I'd bang a cheese sandwich together and pour a glass of milk. That was it. Typing didn't use up many calories. But not so on the river. This was serious business.

Putting the condiments away, I spied a jar of pickled asparagus that immediately found its way into the cooler along with a dozen bottles of ale from Whitefish Brewery, a micro-operation near home operated by a friend. The trout may not cooperate, but at least we wouldn't starve to death today. Thinking ahead (a rare occurrence), I pulled some elk steaks out of the freezer and went out to the grill to lay a fire for tonight. Someday I'd make some woman a dandy little home-maker. The air was still frosty, but warming as the sun climbed higher in the sky. I decided to forego long underwear and stick with hip-waders instead of the neoprenes.

I passed the time reading some more old magazines, mar-veling at the self-important, precious captions to the photographs in *Gray's*. I found it hard to believe that anyone really viewed hunting and fishing in such a self-conscious, stylized manner. They could have the whole attitude. I'll take my crazy friends and a gonzo approach to life any day. No *salmo* spoken here.

Just before noon, I heard Dernier's well-traveled Chevy truck pull up out front—raft loaded, gear stored, ready to go. I tossed my stuff in back and Davalio moseyed over from the bunkhouse and did the same. We piled in and headed for the same put-in as yesterday. Vic had arranged for a friend to drive Bob's truck back later on.

We struck off, passing deer and grouse on the way to the highway that led to Darby and the bridge that gave us access to the river. Bob was a top-notch banjo player and had a Bela Fleck tape going. Up until a couple of years ago, I'd never heard of the guy. Now he was all over the dial. In stores, on PBS, touring, you name it. His demonic talent certainly deserved the recognition. Hell, we all deserved recognition. In one obscure way or another, we were all artists, or so we liked to believe in our delusional lit-tle worlds. Strange mindsets surfacing before high noon.

The day was already in the mid-50s, balmy, at least for March, when we hit the water. Davalio was in front, Dernier manned the oars, and I settled down in back. Mayflies, a few small brown caddis, and an occasional skwala buzzed above the river among the bankside vegetation that crawled among the rocks. Fish were already working steadily in all the usual locations, splashing rises for the emerging caddis. Casual sips for the mayflies and noisy slurps for the stoneflies. I'd never seen this much activity in early spring on the Bitterroot, or any other Montana river. Browns and rainbows all over the place.

Vic was quickly into a brown that had nailed a blue-winged olive. Colorful, fat as usual, and about 17 inches, it rolled and thrashed in the water. I drifted a skwala, my own tie with elk hair caddis overtones, behind Davalio's float and a dark shape sucked in the bug then went straight to the bottom and held its ground. Lifting up on the rod as we passed, and almost on top of the fish, the trout broke loose and ran down stream, stopped, then surfaced and came to net. A brook trout almost black on top with dark blue on the flanks, silvery belly, white-tipped fins, and a few sky-blue spots. Twelve inches and a rarity on this stretch of water.

"What next, Holt? A squawfish or maybe a sucker?" Davalio was always generous with his praise, frequently commenting on my sharp casting, fine floats, or the size of my fish. If I caught a 20-incher he called it a "solid 16." If he caught a 16 it was a "wallhanger." We all had our shortcomings, though mine were very few in number. I'd learned to overlook Vic's, most of the time. After all, he did all of the driving on our numerous and lengthy road trips. He had a nice raft and good taste in wines, and he never bitched when things got tough, as they often do, out in the field. Guys like that and Dernier are not easy to find. A few chinks in the armor, an eccentricity or two, but that was all part of the game.

"At least squawfish are natives. Your brown isn't," I shot back with frightening alacrity while lighting a Camel with a sputtering stick match. Where was my windproof lighter? Buried in a pocket somewhere.

"Hell of a comeback, Holt," Dernier said over his back, giving me a wry grin and a shrug of the shoulders. "I don't know if I can handle an afternoon filled with this level of repartee. The Algonquin Roundtable surfaces on the Bitterroot. Let me go, Lord."

We took browns, rainbows, a westslope cutthroat, and a hybrid in the next mile. Then Davalio and Dernier traded places. Neither one of them trusted me on the oars unless we were floating the zoo that the Bighorn has become. Then I was fair game, forced to bob and weave my way through the armada of drift boats, rafts, and one-man conveyances as we searched for open water. We hadn't been back there in a few years, except during the January thaw when the river was pretty much empty. Otherwise it was a nuthouse crammed with lunatics tagging rainbows on redds, posturing fools crowding others out of pools, greedy guides who could care less about the resource, and even the odd, truly odd, fistfight. Something had gone very wrong on the Horn and we wanted no part of its sickness during the frantic months that ran from March through November. Dernier needed his solitude and refused to fish under these kinds of conditions. A dark, malevolent expression would wash over his face when the subject was brought up. We'd learned to avoid the topic altogether for the sake of tranquillity and a good time while fishing or carousing elsewhere.

I'd known these two for years. Fished and hunted with them every chance I could. Vic Davalio and Bob Dernier were both active in Trout Unlimited, working hard to preserve, and even enhance, the resource. We were all terrified that the country we lived for would be destroyed by developers, invaded by new residents, and stripped away to nothing by the hideous actions of the timber and mining industries—not to mention threats from dewatering by irrigation, ground water pollution, and stream damage from grazing cattle. Bob also guided on the Big Hole just over the mountains to the east. He was on the water 175 days a year. Vic floated friends and special guests at his lodge, but spent most of his time bird and antelope hunting over east, especially in the wide, lonesome Missouri Breaks somewhere by Zortman. None of us could ever get enough of this stuff. We were hopelessly hooked. Flyrods, reels, guns of various calibers and gauge, waders, camping gear, and the like lay scattered around our homes like most normal people arranged furniture. At times it was difficult, and slightly embarrassing to explain the multitudes of equipment to friends and family who did not share our affliction. Such is life.

Up ahead was a nice bucket that Dernier failed to reach, but I managed to drift the skwala right through the middle of the thing. A huge brown slammed the bug and scrambled across slack, shallow water, kicking up gravel and silt as it streaked for a slack pool filled with dense aquatic plants. I failed to check the trout and the 4X leader snapped as the fish twisted around in the weeds, the line shooting in ugly coils back into my lap and over my right arm.

"Great job, again, Holt," Davalio said with a snicker. "Try 0X. Or maybe you should bring a baitcasting outfit next time. That was a hell of a big fish."

Dernier was silent, no doubt thinking about how he would have played the brown. I was quiet, too, while tying on fresh tippet and a new fly; disappointed a bit at not seeing the true size of the trout, but not all that upset. Win some, lose some. There'd be more and Dernier already had a rainbow on, a nice fish that took his pattern as it drifted next to a downed cottonwood that paralleled the current. The fish leaped a little, sounded, leaped once more, then came to net. Dark-spotted with a deep, blood-red band along its sides. A 20-inch male with a developing kype. A fish that was approaching spawning velocity as spring neared. Sometimes rivers seem fishless, dead, and without hope. Yesterday and today were the opposite. The action was constant for large trout. The Bitterroot was showing off and the angling gods were shining down on us with generosity.

We pulled over on a gravel shore next to a long, deep run overhung with alder and willow. Dense root balls provided even more cover. Vic waded out and began working a skwala bank-tight while Bob and I devoured our lunch and offered pithy advice on our friend's presentation technique. He never heard us and was fast into a large brown that snapped his tippet to the root. Our silence said it all. Davalio refused to acknowledge our existence and Bob and I started laughing.

"Cut the serious crap, Davalio. Even Holt could have caught that one."

"Thanks, Bob."

Davalio was soon tight to another brown, this time in more open surroundings a little up stream. The brown rolled in the green-tinged water, and we could see its golden belly as it did so. Then the trout ran under the bank and broke off.

"That's it, Davalio. You can keep rowing. You're making a mess of the river. It's a damn travesty." Dernier tossed a part of his sandwich at him. Vic trudged back to the raft.

"I never did like that damn Rio tippet material. It's too brittle," he complained while digging out a beer and a sandwich from the cooler. "The stuff doesn't have any give to it."

"Cut the jive, Davalio. You blew both fish and you know it." This time a piece of his sandwich came winging my way. Mature adults at the height of sophistication and angling refinement. A pathetic display honed to perfection over the seasons. No rest for the wicked or some such nonsense.

We wound our way down the river. Eagles and hawks soared overhead. A kingfisher spooked at our approach just above a wooden weir where we pulled over to fish. Whitetails were all over the place, as were bunches of chickadees, sparrows, and nuthatches. Bugs continued to hatch. Buds were visible on the trees. The pines were shading from an almost black-green to emerald. The willows were turning bright as the sap began to move up into their limbs. Life was coming back to the Bitterroot in a rush.

We took several small rainbows, all of them 12 inches or so, and a brown of 14 inches in the sapphire water that bubbled like a natural hot tub as it poured over the planked weir. Dernier slid the raft over the obstruction and we drifted on in silence, taking in the day and more browns and rainbows up to 18 inches on skwalas. We never saw another raft or obnoxious one-man Water Otter the entire float. We didn't even see any bankside anglers. The only contact we had with the so-called real world was when the river bent close to the highway where we could hear cars and trucks whiz by, or when we drifted by a farm or home set close to the water. Even with the influx of full- and part-time residents from both out-of-state and from other parts of Montana, the Bitterroot retained its wild character. Except for the westslope cutthroat, the rare bull trout, ubiquitous mountain whitefish, and the dreaded squawfish, the trout population was introduced from stockings in the past. These fish had turned wild decades ago and were now self-sustaining, and providing a quality fishery.

The large rock in midstream across from Davalio's lodge hove into view. Bob took one last cast just above the thing. His fly rode the current, hitting a perfect seam. A rainbow rose up and snatched the bug with a splashing take, then crashed and leapt downstream. The fish was played quickly, brought to the raft, and released. A nice end to a perfect day on the river.

"Well, Holt, you can't bitch about the fishing you've had the last two days," Davalio said as we unloaded our gear. Dernier nodded and looked down river at a pair of geese strutting on a small island, honking and puffing up with indignation at our presence. What was Bob thinking? That old dark look appeared on his face.

Was he seeing a future where the river was hemmed in by subdivisions and overrun with rafts and boats? Was he imaging a time when places like this were nothing more than dim memories tinged with sorrow and longing? Or was he trying to figure out how to mount that AK-47 on the bow of his raft? No quarter asked for. No quarter given. Perhaps.

I hoped the Bitterroot remained forever just like it was today, that people like Dernier and Davalio, my friends, always had magic places such as this one to fish and hunt and, most importantly, to use as a hide-out from the thundering herd.

T·H·R·E·E

Mississagi Breakdown

THIS WAS HARDLY THE WAY TO BEGIN A CANOE trip. My stepfather, Ken, and I took the first small rapid spinning around and careening backward through the foaming water. Our guide, Aaron Proulx, and my stepbrother, Ted, were holding in the pool below us, laughing at our ungainly efforts. The aluminum canoe banged loudly off exposed rocks, the harsh, metallic noise ricocheting off the dense stands of pine and hardwoods that lined the Mississagi. Several loggers, sitting on a bridge near where we put in, offered succinct comments concerning our technique.

"Nice job, eh?" "Try using your paddles, boys." "The front end normally goes first on the river around here," and so on. Ken grinned around a big green cigar, which smoldered on one end and was chewed to a spinach-like appearance on the other. What the hell, any landing you can walk away from.

"Owooga," Ted screeched, and he was really laughing now. "Good job, Dad. I'm glad I'm with the guide. I'm too young to die."

"Going to be an interesting trip, eh, Kenny?" Aaron offered and struck off downstream with deep, powerful strokes from his wide paddle that left miniature whirlpools behind him as he went. We followed as best we could, making good time with the aid of the current despite our ineptitude. Three days of this and I was sure we'd be honed into a well-coordinated rowing machine. Maybe.

I already had my 6-weight rigged with a red and white streamer of indeterminate nature. There were northern pike to a dozen pounds, big brooks, or speckled trout as they are called in this part of Ontario, and a fair number of smallmouth bass. The northerns ate everything in sight, including smaller gamefish. The brookies and bass fed on minnows, frogs, crustaceans, and insects in all their stages of development.

The first cast turned nothing, but the second, which landed next to the rocky bank, was more entertaining. One strip and a pike came out of nowhere and attacked my fly savagely. The fish fought well while Ken tried gallantly to avoid hitting midstream rocks and beached logs. I'm sure the northern had never experienced a ride like this one, as he was dragged downstream like a terrified water-skier being yanked around by a ship of fools. Reaching a calm stretch in the river, I dragged the fish to the canoe, the thing three-quarters dead from drowning. But it swam off quickly when I twisted the hook loose with a pair of pliers. Maybe seven pounds, dark green with tan, oblong spots and a coppery belly. The mouth was filled with row upon row of razor-sharp teeth.

I've caught countless northerns, and have never tired of the sport. The quickness with which they pounce on the fly is almost frightening; swift death on their primitive minds. They fight well, and most times of the year readily take a fly, daredevil, or bait. Search and destroy is their motto.

The species is surrounded in myth and plain old-fashioned BS. The infamous Mannheim pike in the British Isles was supposed to be 267 years old, a bit of a stretch considering the average life span is more like 10. A 350-pound pike of 19 feet was reported taken from Lake Kaiserwag, but the wall mount turned out to be a reconstruction using several large fish. In Bohemia, sighting a pike is considered a bad omen, but then what isn't over there. The largest pike caught are in the 40-pound range, but I've seen much larger ones pulled from the nets belonging to an old Indian on the North Channel of

Lake Huron—*much* bigger. They looked like railroad ties with teeth and eyes and fins.

"Quit your damn fishing and help me paddle," Ken admonished. "I'm working my ass off back here." Turning around, I saw him putting fire to his cigar, the paddle resting across his knees, and a jive grin creasing his face. I couldn't see his eyes; they were hidden behind dark glasses. But I was sure they were sparkling with giving-me-a-hard time intent. A long trip, indeed.

Aaron Proulx had been friends with Ken since childhood when they spent their summers together fishing and screwing around at Ken's family summer home on a small island an hour east of Sault Ste. Marie, Michigan. Now, Proulx only guided for his friends, keeping the best of the rivers and lakes of his country a fairly well-kept secret. He and Ken planned the trip to give my mother and siblings a break from our rambunctious, some would say obnoxious, pranks and free form behavior that manifested itself in a variety of strange activities, which included tossing firecrackers into the night air in hopes of blowing up bats, short-sheeting beds, and running our sister's underwear up the flag pole. Cute kids courting severe beatings or dismemberment. We were basically out of control whenever we got together. Our golden retriever, Northwind, was part of the gang, swimming happily behind our boat as we went off in search of mayhem. Everyone on the island, including the cook, needed a break. Aaron and Ken were brave men. The trip turned out to be the first of several I took with Proulx. That alone made this adventure special as I look back on it from the distance of many years.

We'd put in on the river a few miles above where the Little White joins the Mississagi and planned to float about 30 miles to the stream's outlet in the North Channel not far from the small town of Blind River. This was Canada, where the rivers were wild and rarely fished. Proulx had floated the river many times during his life. He was about 40 as was Ken; Ted and I were in our early teens. Unlike today, the old Mississagi was a pristine stream unspoiled by pollution from logging-caused siltation and leakage from some residential septic systems. You could dip a cup in the river and drink your fill. Gamefish populations were healthy. Today the flow is still a quality fishery, but the pike, bass, and trout have a slightly off-color taste at times, and the water needs to either be boiled or treated with chemical additives. Signs of the times, unfortunately.

Today's stretch was about 10 miles to a campsite on a high rock bank overlooking the river, or so I'd been told. After several miles of easy paddling, we hit smooth water that flowed sluggishly. Steady paddling was required, and after a couple of miles my arms were tired. I couldn't hear Ken behind me except for the occasional sound of his Zippo lighter as he restoked his cigar. Turning around, I again saw the paddle resting on his knees. I'd been doing all of the work with the exception, apparently, of occasional course corrections on Ken's part.

"Don't kill yourself back there."

"Don't worry John Boy. I won't."

I heard the lighter's lid click open then close with a metallic snap.

"Aaron and I are cooking dinner and setting up the tents. We need to conserve our strength."

"Right," I said aloud and "bullshit" under my breath. I could see Proulx paddling away in the distance, while my stepbrother played a fish that turned out to be a nice smallmouth of a pound or two. The bass was derricked into the canoe and plopped into a cooler. A few more and we had dinner.

Another 30 minutes and the river picked up its pace, splashing and racing through, past, and over large golden brown and bluish gray rocks. Plenty of room to float through, so I launched the streamer into likely looking holes, above the rocks, and along deep glides beneath the sheer granite cliffs. Smallmouth were everywhere, racing for a #6 marabou muddler (I'd changed flies earlier) and attacking the pattern in a rush, then pulling hard for cover. The species is a superb quarry and fights harder pound-for-pound than trout, char, northerns, or largemouth bass. The first one I took was about two pounds and fought like a bulldog. These things were strong.

Smallmouths have been taken to twelve pounds or so, but a five-pounder is a trophy anywhere. Proulx said he and his father had taken them to six pounds on this river. I wanted one of those in the worst way.

"Nice fish John Boy. Catch some more. We can have the steaks tomorrow."

"Just watch where you're going. I did my share of the work already."

"Oh, oh. The fly fisherman is getting upset."

I heard the damned Zippo fire up again.

Ken and I got along great, were growing into friends, but he knew how to push my buttons. It wasn't so much what he said, it was when and how he said things. I ignored him and went back to fishing, noticing while I did so that both Ted and Proulx had fish on and then so did I.

This one was a two-pounder that wagged its head, sending spray in all directions, before the bass raced toward the far side of the river and some exposed maple tree roots. I checked the fish and landed him after a couple of minutes of iron-hard, determined struggle. This was well before the hideous days of political correctness that is now practiced by the new legions of *effete* flyfishers everywhere. They seem to be unaware that fishing is a blood sport. There is a place for releasing the majority of fish one connects with, but to never kill and eat a wild gamefish, to at least have the choice of life or death, reduces fly fishing, all fishing, to a sterile, juiceless exercise in nothing. Nothing more than a stylized circle jerk. The yupsters could cast my way all the aspersions they wished. They're flotsam.

The campsite came into view as we zipped through a narrow chute of foamy water that poured light brown, tinged with tannin from pine needles that fell into the river. A narrow trail climbed to a spacious, moss-covered area about 20 feet above the water. We hauled our gear up there, and in what seemed like just a couple of minutes, camp was set up and a nice fire was going strong. While Ted and I foraged downed limbs from the forest, Ken made drinks for Aaron and himself. Cocktail hour.

We kids went down to the river and cleaned the small-mouth—eight of them—green and bronze colored with a black band along their flanks. Their stomachs were filled with crayfish, minnows, beetles, and what looked like caddis and stonefly nymphs. We filleted the fish, the flesh a translucent white, and tossed the remains into the woods for marauding raccoons. Proulx was frying up sliced potatoes and onions in a large cast-iron skillet. I was starved and the rich aroma of the mixture made my stomach growl in anticipation. Another pan was placed on the fire and loaded with cooking oil. The fillets were dredged in a mixture of ground cornmeal, salt and pepper, and placed in the hot oil. The fish immediately sizzled and turned brown in a hurry. Proulx dished out four healthy portions and all was silence except for the sounds of enthusiastic eating, like a pack of wolves at a fresh kill. The bass were crispy on the outside and sweet and juicy on the inside. The potatoes and onions were cooked perfectly, seasoned with plenty of freshly-ground pepper and some salt. A simple meal that rivaled anything served by a fancy, nose-in-the-air restaurant. The river flowing along provided the background music. A pair of blue jays appeared above us, perched on an overhanging limb. They eagerly anticipated an unexpected meal. Not much, if any, food remained when we finished eating. Just scraps that the beggar birds snared from the ground as soon as we pitched them behind us in the woods. The two birds made quite a racket as they fought over each choice morsel. Ken and Proulx relaxed over coffee and some Courvoisier while the galley crew trudged down to the river to do the dishes. Youth has its disadvantages.

Once finished, Ted and I headed off downriver in search of mischief, which we found in the form of a gang of small frogs croaking and leaping among the slippery rocks. Back home we chased girls. Out here we chased frogs. What can I say?

The mid-July night was cooling off rapidly, and we moved to the fire to warm up from our riverine peregrinations and to avoid the few mosquitoes that hummed around us. An early morning was on the schedule, so we soon went off to our tent and a good night's sleep.

The next morning, Aaron already had the fire going, coffee brewing, bacon sizzling, orange juice made, and more potatoes frying when I heaved to around 5:30. Silently, he pointed out a bull moose that was feeding on some lush grass across the river, the massive animal tearing large clumps of the plants, roots and all, from the muck. I could hear it munching as water from the stuff sloshed from the sides of its square snout.

Eeeehoow, Eeehoow scratched across the crisp air. Proulx, hands cupped around his mouth, was directing this slightly ludicrous sound toward the moose, who stopped eating and slowly lifted its head, the huge rack turning back and forth as the creature tried to determine where the call was coming from. *Eeehow, Eeehow.* Higher pitched this time. The moose took two steps into the river, spied us, stared for a few, long seconds, then turned and trotted into the woods, vanishing from sight in a flash.

"What was that supposed to mean to the moose?" I asked.

"It's something of a territorial call," Proulx said. He placed the bacon on a plate and then cracked a dozen eggs into the hot grease, which smoked and hissed and sent a thin cloud of steam upward.

"I didn't want him around when we put in later. The bulls can be damn aggressive, eh?"

I poured a cup of coffee as Ken and Ted made ragged appearances.

"What the hell was all the racket?" my stepfather asked. "Calling the damn moose again, Aaron? That's one of his little parlor tricks he drags out to amuse his friends. After 30 years it's getting a bit stale, Aaron."

"The moose didn't think so. Eat your breakfast. You've got a big day ahead of you smoking those stinking cigars and watching John paddle," and he flashed me a private wink.

"Holding on to those things must wear a man out by day's end, I'd imagine. You'd better watch yourself. We're a long way from the nearest hospital. Twenty miles at least."

Ken grunted and worked over his breakfast as we all did. Then we broke camp and set off down the Mississagi with the sun just beginning to crest the trees as we hit the water.

"The next few miles are pretty fast. All you have to do is steer. There's a nasty rapid where two rock shelves squeeze the river tight. We'll pull in above and I'll run the canoes through myself. You can't take this one backwards, Kenny."

Small mayflies, #14 or thereabouts, climbed off the water. White Millers? Smallmouths and brook trout rose side by side to take in the delicate bugs. I tied on a White Wulff, greased the sucker up, and began casting to the fish. They weren't particular, taking my fake with the same gusto as they pounced on the naturals. The brookies were eager but not much in the way of fighters. A quick run and then I dragged them to net. Twelve to fourteen inches, dark blue, faded red spots circled by soft turquoise, yellowish-orange fins tipped with white and black. Light gold vermiculations along their flanks. Their colors were muted this time of year, not lit up as they would be in a couple of months for spawning. But they were still gorgeous fish, and I released them all and the smallmouths, too.

Steak was on the menu tonight. The bass had completed their procreational imperative about a month earlier and had fully recovered from the rigors of their mating dance. They'd regained lost weight and were firm and thick-bodied. The same held true for a pair of northerns that I connected with in a large pool an hour later while waiting for Proulx to drive the canoes through the churning cut he'd mentioned earlier. Both pike were about eight pounds and fought like living rockets, racing with current before turning sideways and making slow runs toward shore.

This was an excellent fishing river. I had to give Ken credit, though it hurt to do so. If you couldn't catch fish here, you were either spastic or dead. I kept casting, taking fish after fish while Ken navigated with a few strokes and gentle pressure on his paddle, a natural wrapper of Cuban lineage clenched in his teeth. This was the good life, much better than harassing the cook or my sister.

I spotted a couple more moose along the way, a golden eagle sailing far overhead, kingfishers, crows, small squirrels that leaped from limb to limb fearlessly, and a number of reddish-tan whitetails. A person would be hard pressed to starve out here. Wildflowers in blues, reds, whites, and oranges dotted the intense green moss. The day was cloudless and the sun was turning the air from cool to warm to hot. I shed my wool shirt, then my t-shirt. A little sunburn action here in Canada. The morning sped by with the enthusiasm of the river's current, and in what seemed only minutes since breakfast, we pulled into a small gravel bay for lunch. Apparently, Mississagi time ain't no relation to nasty, big-city time.

As always, food outdoors takes on a heightened importance. On the menu today were moose meat sandwiches on homemade bread (it seemed that they were everywhere in various forms around here). There was also a bag of carrots, ice-cold bottles of Molson's ale (Ted and I even got one each), and fudge brownies for dessert. Then back to the river and four more miles filled mainly with brook trout.

Even Ken launched a few casts, taking some nice trout, one of 16 inches that was so husky it must have weighed a couple of pounds. He had switched to a pipe for the afternoon's labors, puffing away as he worked a small black-nosed dace along the shore while mumbling "beautiful" or "come on little fishies." He'd been flyfishing for years, since the late '30s, and made the whole process look so easy; a casual observer might have thought that there was nothing to the sport. In a run-turned pool, he hooked a small brookie and was bringing it to him when a dark-green submarine torpedoed out of the Stygian depths and swallowed the hapless trout. This took all of us by surprise, certainly the brook trout was somewhat shocked. The large northern ran down below us before tearing up the river's surface next to Ted and Proulx. The large head wagged back and forth, pink water spraying from its gills and jaws. Then the thing sounded and held tight along the bottom, allowing us to gain ground. Finally, I could see him holding in the weak current. A log of a fish, perhaps 15 pounds or more, Ken tried to lift it, but the rod bent double and the northern stayed put: a standoff while I held the canoe in place. A few more attempts with the same results, then for reasons known only to the pike, it shot straight up through the river, clearing the water easily before crashing back down on the leader, which snapped with a sickening *crack*. We were all stunned and disappointed, but still excited with the rush of putting the hook into such a maniac fish.

"Jesus. You see the size of the thing," I stammered.

Ken just worked on his pipe, thick smoke curling around his head.

"Well, Kenny," Proulx said. "Looks like you lost dinner for us again. How many times on this river does that make? And I didn't know you liked to use the damn bait for your fishing. Those speckled trout work nice, eh."

We floated on for an hour or so before reaching another gravel bay with a long, wide beach that sloped ever so gradually toward a stand of cedar. A perfect place to camp, and I was starved for some rare, red meat. Proulx, with slight help from us, again had camp set up, a fire going and potatoes frying in mere minutes—in an instant was more like it. Ken built Canadian whiskey and water drinks with a couple of cubes bobbing gaily in the metal cups. Ted and I crashed next to the fire and sipped another Molson, which Proulx had plucked from a cooler and tossed to us. Under age, but so what? The beer tasted good, better than it ever tasted when I was an adult. This was hard to beat. Ken pulled out a four-pound beef fillet from another cooler and worked a splash of cognac into the meat before rubbing it with crushed cloves of garlic and a dusting of Coleman's dried mustard. A little ground pepper and the slab was ready to burn. Boy, life was brutal on this river.

After devouring our meal, we gathered wood for the night's fire and settled in. The sky glowed flaming orange and yellow then shaded from light blue to purple overhead. A gentle wind worked down from the rocky hills behind, rustling the pines and leafy trees. Mayflies and the odd caddis floated off the river, and talk turned to fishing and hunting, as it always does in camp at this time of day.

I'd only caught a few muskies in my life and those came from the waters around Presque Isle in northern Wisconsin. I asked if there were any around here and Proulx said that there were some in a chain of lakes about 20 air miles to the northwest. Nothing big, perhaps to 18 pounds, but they were easy to catch on large streamers.

The lakes drained a large expanse of swamp that was difficult to get to, especially now that a booming population of beavers had damned most of the outlets, which raised water levels over abandoned logging roads. Early in the year, hordes of mosquitoes and swarms of black flies turned the experience into an ordeal the last time he was there. Proulx added that a wealthy executive from the Canadian Pacific Railroad had built a large log lodge on the shore of one of the lakes in the early '20s, but the place was empty now and slowly sinking into the soggy ground. It was a place shrouded in mystery and purported to be haunted by the ghost of a logger who was killed when a widow-maker fell and crushed his skull. A friend of Proulx' claimed to have run into the apparition with terrifying results and absolutely refused to come near the flowage. As is a guide's calling, tales around a crackling fire as darkness closes in are part of the package. This is his friend's tale as recounted that second night on the Mississagi:

Perley Sauvage paddled smoothly along the shore of the third lake in a chain of seven, the largest of the group that were all connected by a tea-colored stream that wound through boggy meadows and dense stands of cedar. He'd put in at an old wooden bridge built in the '20s to access some virgin timber on a distant ridge. The road was overgrown with grass, weeds, and small pines. Only the occasional hunter or fisherman wandered up this way and these were mostly locals who knew about the huge moose and abundant numbers of muskies that lived here. Sauvage was wandering through the region looking for moose, and looking to catch some of the muskies using his stout baitcasting rod and large red and white daredevils. The canvas canoe, patched many times over the years, was loaded down with camping and fishing gear, foodstuffs, and a battered lever-action 30-30 that his father gave to him years ago. There were a few hours to sunset; plenty of time to work the coves and points of the lake before gliding over to the lodge to make camp next to the ramshackle front porch of the lodge. Musky Lodge its owner called it, though the sign proclaiming this fact was gone, probably stolen for a souvenir or used as kindling by a hunting party.

He cast the spoon tight to shore and reeled it in swiftly but not for long. A large fish smashed the metal imitation. Sauvage pulled back with force on the rod, driving the sharp treble hooks deep into the fish's jaws. The stab of the points galvanized the musky, Sauvage could see that now as the fish tore up the surface of the still lake. Charging back and forth not far from shore, the musky refused to give up the fight. Ten minutes passed, and even with 15-pound test line Sauvage played the fish carefully, fearing that the razor sharp rows of teeth would saw through the line. Eventually the musky tired and rolled on its belly, exhausted, allowing itself to be reeled in. Sauvage pulled an old Colt .22 revolver from his canvas pack and popped the fish twice in the head. The musky thrashed once, quivered, then died.

Sauvage grabbed it by the tail before carefully pulling the spoon free. Careless fishermen had brought muskies into their boats not yet dead with hooks exposed only to have the maddened fish break into a frenzy of thrashing that inevitably embedded one or more of the hooks into a calf muscle or a thumb. A bloody, painful experience never forgotten, but this fish was stone-cold dead. Large enough to provide several pounds of meat for dinner along with some wild rice and a little bourbon mixed with the lake water that held the taste of pine.

Sauvage paddled to the lodge, set up camp, gathered a large cache of wood and built a fire. The whiskey tasted cold and warm at the same time as it worked away in his stomach. He'd already gutted the fish, finding it full of minnows, and a small, partially-digested rodent, probably a baby beaver. He scaled the fish and cut it into steaks as one would with a salmon, then he dredged the flesh in a mixture of flour, corn-meal, and salt and placed the hunks on an enamel-coated plate. Large chunks of salt pork sizzled in an oversized frying pan. He loved its salty taste, and the grease gave the fish an excellent flavor. Whiskey and the meat, that was all he desired. He leaned back against his pack watching the fire and working on his drink, a good day now shading into dusk. The land was his life, the way he made money and passed the days. Hunting, fishing, trapping, even harvesting wild rice by beating the native grain with his paddle on the gunwale of his canoe; he earned enough to supply simple needs. He lived primarily off the land. A free man.

Sauvage pounded down the fried musky, scrapped the leavings in the fire and settled back with another whiskey, his feet close to the fire. The lodge loomed just to his left, shutters hanging at odd angles alongside shattered windows. The night breeze whistled eerily through gaps in the logs and around corners of the old building. He wasn't afraid of the dark or the animals that used the darkness as cover when they foraged in the woods. He could hear them now. Small ones scampering across the duff and larger ones stepping through the trees.

Making a last drink, his attention turned to the lodge. A faint, blue glow was moving from room to room on the second floor, a light barely flickering from window opening to opening.

"Strange, that is," he thought, and grabbed his flashlight to investigate. No one was here, he was sure of that. Stepping carefully across the rotted boards of the porch, he entered the doorway, the door itself lay on the floor covered with dust and needles. Ratty furniture filled the great room, discarded, worthless in its advanced state of decay. The owner had removed the paintings that used to cover the walls along with things like silver and dishware and other easily transported valuables. Pack rats lurched for cover when exposed to the beam of his light. The air inside here was cool, almost icy. Sauvage shivered. A slow dragging sound came from the room above him. He patted the pistol he'd tucked into the front of his pants, then turned and started up the rickety stairs. The carved banister wobbled when he put any weight on it. A board cracked under his foot. The going was slow and hazardous, and a false step could mean a cut, a sprained ankle, or worse. A low, moaning came from the hallway. The wind?—a touch of something uncomfortable, not familiar, crossed over him. Something wasn't right here.

A tremendous crashing started on the steps above him, sounds of splintering wood and a heavy object crashing down. Pushing the banister over, he leaped to the first floor as a massive leather chair tumbled past. The thing would have squashed him like a bug if he hadn't jumped. Covered in dust and debris, he stood up shakily and brushed off the sleeves of his wool sweater and pulled the gun out. He was afraid now, but had never backed down from anything in his life. He wouldn't start tonight.

Working his way cautiously up the stairs one more time, he could see the track of the chair in the thick dust, skid marks and shattered wood along the pine paneling and down the steps. At the top, an old portrait of someone in early-19th century naval garb hung at an angle backed by peeling wallpaper. Sauvage could imagine why the painting had been left behind. Who would want that silly bastard in their home with the dark eyes following every move you made? And that garish gold-plated frame. "Money can't buy good taste, eh, Sauvage," he said out loud. A long hallway went both left and right, leading to bedrooms, he guessed. The light had come from the right, so he started slowly in that direction.

His hands felt clammy and he was perspiring, something he rarely did even when cutting trees down by hand. He turned off the flashlight in hopes of locating the mysterious glow. He did. A crease of light almost flowed from a crack in a doorway near the end of the hall. Soft moaning, an unearthly sound, reached him. Moving slowly now with the gun pointed straight ahead, he was almost there when a translucent shape exited the room and wavered not 10 feet from him.

The vision was over six feet tall and Sauvage could just make out knee-high, laced boots and a plaid shirt. The thing's head, its hideous appearance, made his knees buckle. Even as soft and hazy as the apparition was, he could easily make out the smashed skull, the eye hanging from its socket by a ragged thread of muscle, blood oozing down the chin, and the clump of brains splattered over a cheek. Sauvage wanted to run but could not move his legs to save his life. The diaphanous sight slid back into the room beckoning as it went and Sauvage followed, hypnotized, and no longer in control. With all his will, he fought to stay out of that room. But his feet led him down and dragged him across the threshold into an ice-cold atmosphere that was at once both devoid of illumination and bright enough to make out a table, bed, a pair of matching Queen Anne chairs, cracked mirror, and another military portrait. The vision appeared once more half-in and half-out of an inside wall.

Something sharp, unyielding, and heavy struck his forehead and Sauvage fell to the floor in a formless heap, out cold.

Sunlight pouring through an open window brought Sauvage around. He lay on the floor in the dust and scattered mouse droppings. Birds were chirping away outside, and he could see a cloudless sky from his prostrate position. Above him hung a heavy chain with the jagged remains of a brass light fixture that dangled from the last link. "Damn thing must of conked me on the head." Standing up slowly, turning dizzy as the blood rushed from his head, he noticed that his pants were damp, from a fearful voiding of his bladder, no doubt. Looking around the room, he saw that nothing of last night's madness remained. Had he dreamed all this? He'd only had a few drinks, and whiskey had never made him hallucinate before. "Time to get the hell out of this crazy damn place," he said, and he did by walking quickly down the hall, taking the steps two at a time, and breaking through the next to last, which laid a cut across his shin. He never stopped, breaking camp in a flash and paddling for all he was worth up the lake and to his truck parked by the road. He tore down the rutted lane in a cloud of blue oil smoke and spinning tires, vowing never to return to the lake and Musky Lodge.

"That's what my friend said happened, and he's not a man to tell stories. He wouldn't lie to me," said Proulx as he stirred the fire with a stick. "You never know what can happen in these woods. Things happen that we can't explain, I think."

The story told in daylight over coffee in a cafe would seem laughable. But, out here, miles from civilization, Sauvage's experience seemed real. Sounds in the trees behind me took on new meaning, and I jumped when an animal broke a twig out there in the dark. Ted and I went off to bed, and Ken and Proulx had a last drink before turning in. Tomorrow and sunrise could not come soon enough for me. Foolish as it all seems now, I was easily spooked by things like the doings at Musky Lodge.

Early the next morning we loaded up and hit the river. We still had about eleven miles to go before we hit the North Channel. The river flowed with enthusiasm on this last pitch, perhaps in eager anticipation of its merger with Lake Huron. In late summer and early fall, chinook salmon ran several miles upstream in a mostly false spawn. The salmonids were planted in the Great Lakes years ago, made a strong effort, and are now providing excellent sport. Proulx said that the fish were easy pickings with "dayglo" egg patterns in the river above its mouth. He also said that some steelhead and large browns also moved into the river during the year, mainly autumn. While not the fighters of their true anadromous relatives that spent years fighting for their lives in the ocean and turning extremely powerful in the process, these fish still had spirit that was worth connecting with. A 10-pound fish is a 10-pound fish in my eyes.

Ken steered while I cast a streamer. I wanted one decent northern to bring home for our cook, Ella; she had a way of turning a pike into a gourmet feast in our wood stove. Anyone who says northerns are not fine table fare has never tasted one prepared by Ella along with her homemade sticky buns and twice-baked potatoes. I cast with enthusiasm taking several fish of five and six pounds. I could see the lake ahead and slightly below us now. Not much time to catch supper, but the old last-cast magic worked its voodoo number and a large northern slammed the fly about a hundred yards from the lake. The fish ran down into the open water and we followed. With no obstructions and very little current, landing the pike was routine out there. The northern went an easy 10 pounds, more like 12. Plenty for dinner. Ken killed it with a blow to the skull with a hand ax and the trip was finished. A glorious time and I wanted to start all over again, right away, only farther upstream this time. We drove to our boat docked in a bay at the little town of Desbarats (pronounced de-bo-rah), loaded our gear, said thanks and good-bye to Proulx, and motored back to the island and warm showers.

Early the next week, Proulx pulled up in his Peterborough coupled with a 9½-horse motor. A great little craft built to perfection with fine wood planking. The engine was ideally matched and would push the boat down the lake at a rapid clip. He asked if I still wanted to go out into the channel and meet Fred Elking, a native Indian who worked a long set of nets between Cedar and Thessalon Islands. I said, "You bet," and off we went. The ride lasted about 40 minutes and along the way we ran past numerous small islands of granite, covered with tall pines and scrub brush around the shorelines. There were submerged reefs all over the place, sharp rock that could and did tear out the bottoms of boats that strayed from safe water. Proulx knew the lay of the lake by heart and scarcely looked around, focusing instead on the open water ahead.

A northwest wind kicked up three-foot waves that the Peterborough rode with ease and elegance, surfing the crests

and gliding down into the troughs and up again as smooth as
silk. Proulx cut the motor and we drifted into Elking's long,
wide wooden dock. Nets were hanging from poles, and Elking
was nowhere in sight. His large boat was gone, but I could
hear it chugging in the lake behind Thessalon along with the
steady chugging of an engine that Proulx said was used to haul
in the nets and fish. An old, weathered cabin was perched on
flat rock beneath the shelter of wind-battered trees. Small out
buildings were located with no apparent master plan. A canoe
and small boat were pulled well up on the smooth rock shore.
The place smelled of fish. Gulls screeched and yelled in the air
above us. White droppings coated the dock and the rocks. Fish
scales sparkled in the sun, embedded in the coarse wood. A
banged-up Savage 12-gauge was leaning against a dock piling,
shells, spent and full, were piled in a wood box nearby. Several
dead birds floated in the oily water surrounded by clumps of
feathers. Elking hated gulls, Proulx let me know, and blasted
away at the birds throughout the day all year long. He was one
of the few people who lived up here that was crazy enough to
stay on an island year round.

Elking loaded up on moose and deer meat along with
the few fish he didn't bring to market in the Sault. He piled in
the whiskey and tins of Three Castles tobacco, too, and said
screw the world. I could appreciate the approach, but would
opt for some form of TV reception being a child of the modern
age. Aside from that, a good stereo and a couple of dogs would
be the only other additions I would make to Elking's setup.

We wandered to the lee of the small, five-acre island. There
was a small pond of about a half-acre just behind the cabin
(more of a catch basin than anything else), but the water was
clear with lily pads and duck weed growing in the shallows. I
could see Elking hauling in the last of his nets, then his boat
making a white, foamy wave as it went. In minutes he was
pulling up to the dock with practiced skill, the weathered craft
sliding to a stop with a gentle bumping of the tires both on
the boat and dock. The swell from the wake washed against
the stern.

"Eh, Proulx brought the kid you told me about with ya, I see. Tall one, ain't he?" Elking coughed around the stub of a brown cigar and began dumping his catch into a pen constructed at the end of the pier. A long cleaning table was next to this. Gulls whirled overhead making a deafening racket: sounds of the sea here far inland.

Walleyes of 10 pounds or more. Large chinook. Some smallmouth and rock bass. Jumbo perch and loads of northerns. A banquet. A real freshwater haul. Based on prices I'd observed at Pendleton's Fish Market in Bruce Mines, I could see why Elking was known to be a wealthy (and frugal) man.

"I saved the best for last, kid." What I saw next stopped me dead in my tracks.

I'd heard tales of big northern pike—40 pounds or more—that swam in deep water and preyed on smaller gamefish. I'd taken several to 25 pounds (so 40 never seemed far-fetched), but the pair Elking hefted onto the deck were monsters. Over five feet and thick. They were aqua-green with creamy markings and the merest hint of orange in the tail and fins. Protective coloring that blended in with the channel. Dark pupils surrounded with red-orange irises. These were true predators, and the bigger of the two quivered slightly, its muscles convulsing along the broad flanks as it struggled through the final stages of death. I lifted the smaller one, barely. It was heavy, solid, and slippery.

"What would these things weigh?" I asked, never taking my eyes from the northerns.

"The hen is the bigger one, and she'll push 60 pounds like she was standin' still. That old boy weighs about five pounds less," said Elking while lighting a fresh cigar. "I've taken them in the spring around 100 goddamned pounds, but they taste no damn good, so I smoke them and feed 'em to the dog.

The pike lying at my feet, was probably a world record, as if that sort of nonsense meant anything to anyone but an insecure yahoo from the city. And right then and there, I promised myself a trip up here in the spring.

Proulx noticed my excitement and smiled. We chatted some more and then departed after delivering some mail picked up in town and a case of whiskey. Elking waved a knife in our direction by way of good-bye, blood-red up past his elbows as he sliced his catch from stem to stern. He wasn't much for talking when there was work to be done, so we left him to his chore. Proulx took me out to Thessalon several more times that summer and I got to know the fisherman as much as anyone could get to know a hermit, an individual who brooked absolutely no bullshit. He even invited me up in early May to see the real northerns, but I'd have to earn my keep. No problem there.

That was the first year I got to know Proulx. Over the ensuing years, he has shown me many more special waters like the Mississagi and men like Elking. I've learned more woodcraft, more patience, and more about myself from him than almost anyone I've ever known. He's 70 now but still hunts, traps, and runs his favorite rivers. He's in better shape than ever, and I plan to drive east from Montana next year along the Trans-Canadian Highway, through Alberta, Saskatchewan, Manitoba, and on into Ontario to visit Proulx, to talk about good country, crazed moose, ghosts, and big pike. But mostly to float the Mississagi one last time with my friend.

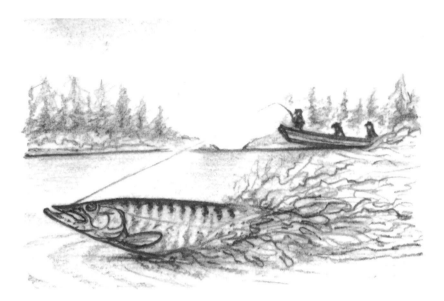

F · O · U · R

Coulee Hats
and Bare Feet
in the North Woods

WE ALL HAVE GONE BAREFOOT on occasion during the wandering course of our lives. I'm in my mid 40s, no longer a kid except in my mind, and I still spend most of the summer shoeless. That's just the way it is. But to walk around in the middle of a brutally cold winter in northern Wisconsin wearing nothing more than chinos, a long-sleeved shirt (a minor concession to the elements) and a coulee hat strikes me, at the very least, as eccentric and downright foolish. I used to know someone who thought nothing of this weird attire, never gave the outfit a second thought. He's dead now, not from hypothermia or frozen feet as you might expect. Old age, cigarettes, and a drink or two finally nailed Cuno Barragan at the peak of life—in his late 70s. He couldn't complain. From what I knew of the guy, he'd lived a full, adventurous, chaotic life, traipsing around the woods and waters in the Boulder Junction and Presque Isle region.

Barragan was born in Minocqua around 1910. By the time he was in his late 20s he'd earned a reputation as one of the state's top guides for walleye and musky. He was also considered a world-class ladies' man, which I'd heard from countless people over the years, but that comes later. Why he disdained the wearing of shoes (he did wear thick-soled moccasins when

61

hunting) no one seems to know. Cuno just kept getting weirder and weirder as the years rolled by. But, he wasn't alone as far as strange behavior went; the Northwoods were and are full of social malcontents who would never pass muster in the big city. The ding-dongs that inhabit the likes of LA had nothing on some of the boys up this way; abnormal behavior was par for the course, and Barragan was the spiritual leader to some extent.

I'd first met the guy in the late '60s while on a long week-end that entailed skipping a few days of high school down south. A friend and I stayed at his father's retreat located on a narrow peninsula jutting out on an isolated lake north of Boulder Junction. We were after walleyes, muskies, grouse, woodcock, and whitetails—anything we could get our hands on or hooks into or gunsights zeroed-in on. We were quite secure in the knowledge that our early November foray was not going to fly with the school's principal, but who cared. A little down time after school copying pages from a dictionary seemed a reasonable price to pay for some free-form adventure. We both had fake IDs, but no one up here gave a damn about the legal age anyway.

One night after taking a limit of grouse along with a couple of woodcock that lacked the innate sense to push off down south with their kin ahead of winter, we strolled into the Presque Isle Inn, a typical Wisconsin tavern of indeterminate lineage: long wooden bar, mirror, mounts of fish and animals all over the place, a juke box featuring the latest hits from Patsy Cline, Hank Williams (the real one, not his boorish offspring), The Andrews Sisters...and a quarter pool table in back that showed more scratched slate than green felt. We ordered a couple of beers, Chief Oshkosh for me and Point for my friend. High class all the way.

Snow and sleet were spitting outside, and the stuff was starting to stick when Barragan walked in. I'd only met him once before, but my friend had filled me in on a few of the local stories. Cuno was about six feet-two and stocky with a tan that did not entirely conceal a ruddy complexion fueled by a nose for booze. His wide, flat feet slapped on the wet wood floor.

They were scarred and heavily callused. The coulee hat was cinched beneath his chin and melting snow leaked over the brim. By this stage of his career, Barragan was in his 60s and he looked it, though he also appeared to be in excellent shape.

"Double of Kessler's and a longneck Old Style," he said in a deep, raspy voice. He plunked down a pack of Kool smokes, pulled an ashtray within hailing distance and settled in for the duration. Closing time was two and it was a little after seven bar time according to the Hamm's clock that ran a never-ending panorama of pristine lakes and green pine forests. The Hamm's bear grinned with learned idiocy off to one side. The Land of Sky Blue Waters, indeed.

Stu and I drilled our beers and ordered another round along with some pickled pig's feet, a bag of pretzels, and a handful of Slim Jims. Eating a good dinner after a long day outdoors was important.

I fired up a Marlboro, and Stu ignited a White Owl that smelled like a wet dog. The good life followed us everywhere. Our first day up here away from the ridiculous boredom that masqueraded as education at Hononegah High. Thank God this was our last year listening to insufferable fools drone on about the Magna Carta, and Illinois State Constitution, and coefficients of linear expansion. Jesus-God it was awful. We left in the dark and got here six hours later, throwing our gear on the living room floor and then heading off to hunt. Tramping all afternoon through the woods and shooting a little and hitting a gamebird every now and then was a release from the tedium that is public education. If it weren't for a healthy population of nubile and eager female classmates, we would have gone stark, raving mad and no doubt turned to robbing gas stations as a form of release. But there's nothing like a cold beer and a good pig's foot to relax a soul. I felt at ease. Stu was hiding behind a pair of aviator sunglasses, hunched over his beer, and munching on a Slim Jim.

Blarp. BLAAARRP.

"Christ. Who died?" I asked Stu.

"Cuno just finished his beer," my friend explained. He'd been coming up here with his family since he was three and knew all of the locals on a first-name basis. Hell, he was ratty enough and crazy enough to be a considered a local himself. "He'll down the whiskey now and order another round. That's how he drinks. He's okay. It's when he shifts to Wild Turkey that things can get a little hairy."

Blarp. BLAAARRP.

"Round two was a technical knockout from the sound of it," said Stu blowing smoke across the bar.

"God those things smell awful. Where'd you find them, in Ole's gym locker?"

"Quality is an acquired taste, Holt. You ain't got it."

"How 'bout a little nine-ball, Stewart?" asked Barragan through eyes shining the faintest of reds. "Say for a round a game?"

"Sure."

"Who's the weasel dick next to you? Sure is a skinny sucker."

"You fished with him last summer for bass over at Dairyman's. Don't remember anything, do you, Cuno," Stu offered and pointed at our bottles for another couple of beers and a setup for Barragan.

Barragan leaned forward and looked down the bar at me, squinting as he did so, the coulee hat tilted at a rakish angle. I took a long pull on my bottle. Beer didn't come any better than the Chief, unless it happened to be Alpine at 79 cents a six, or the legendary product that made Monroe, Wisconsin, forgettable: Huber Brewing Company's renowned Hi-Brau Beer at 14 cents a quart plus.

"He's the idiot that fell out of the canoe trying to cast that damn fly rod of his. Jesus, what a sight. Sounded like someone had dropped a log in the lake. Thought he was going under for real on that one. Swims about as well as a two-legged pup, too."

We went back to the table armed with drinks and quarters. The table was a classic. The felt was either ripped or missing. The rails were pockmarked with cigarette burns, and the balls were chipped and faded. You needed a sand wedge here to have any chance.

Cuno racked them up in a diamond formation, and Stu broke without any success. Then Cuno popped the cue ball into the one and off the table, the off-white sphere rolled erratically along the hardwood wood before exiting the bar and careening into the men's room. We could hear the ball rattle around on the tile floor in there for long seconds, then silence, then Stu went in and retrieved the thing. The sound of running water and paper towels came next, then Stu with a clean ball.

"Nailed the urinal, Cuno. Never missed one in your life, have you?" said Stu making no effort to stifle his laughter. "Drive six hours to fetch a cue ball out of a bar pisser. Thing should work fine, though. It's nice and chilled from the ice they dump in there. Where's the one ball?"

Stu directed the conversation to muskies, asking Cuno if they were on the move over by Crab Lake and, if so, what should we use.

"Hell, a three-horse motor works fine. Damn things attack the prop. They think its a wounded walleye or sucker," coughed Barragan. "Don't let the warden catch you trolling with a motor. Cost me 50 bucks last year, for a damn fish. Tell you what. Meet me in town tomorrow and I'll take you to a place where they are thick as thieves. Your friend can even bring his fly rod. I don't see the big deal with fly fishing, anyway. We used to use bamboo on the Chippewa River for muskies in the '30s. Seemed like more trouble than it was worth. The sight of him falling in the lake again will be worth my time. Big damn fish in there. Thirty pounds or more. Swampy. Not many bother. Plan on bringing hip waders and dress warm. Bring a rifle. We can pop a buck on the way out."

Now that the next day was taken care of, we turned our attentions to the pool table, where a strange game was turning. The balls pretty much went where they wanted, skipping and bouncing across the surface. We played until closing, each of us winning and losing more or less equally. An unstable table behind us was covered with beer bottles and glasses when that most dreaded of all dreaded words were issued by the bartender.

"Last call."

Each of us shivered involuntarily.

Stu and I ordered beers and shots all around. These we downed with dispatch and we headed our separate ways. We'd meet Barragan in town around eight the next morning.

On the way home, about two inches of wet snow were on the ground making the highway slick. Deer were thick along the side of the road on the way in, eyes glowing orange in our headlight beams like miniature lamps. Dead ones, smashed by logging trucks and other vehicles lay in bloody, mangled heaps in the ditches. There were so many animals in the state, they'd become a hazard to travel. Either that or they starved to death. Once home, I crashed in my sleeping bag on the floor in front of a hastily-built fire and Stu collapsed on a couch.

In the morning, one that broke clear and in the low 30s, we filled two thermos jugs with thick, black coffee, loaded the necessary gear, and made the run into town and Lefty's Cafe. Lefty was actually a righty who'd lost his arm in a hunting accident a long time ago. Barragan was seated at a table by the window working over a stack of pancakes drenched in maple syrup and butter. A plate of ham, four eggs, and hash browns covered in ketchup was nearby. We ordered the same in somewhat weaker proportions and sipped some strong coffee. Three box lunches were also secured. Roast beef sandwiches, candy bars, chips, and homemade doughnuts. When our food came, we ate in silence, left a tip, grabbed the lunches, and paid the bill.

Outside, Cuno said only that we were to follow him to the lake. It was a long drive where the pavement gave way to gravel, then dirt. Small streams and large lakes flickered between gaps in the forest. Again, the deer were out, despite it being hunting season. Nothing big. Nothing worth shooting. Barragan turned off on a two-lane affair that was filled with water in the low spots. We got out and locked the hubs of the

Scout before proceeding in four-wheel drive. Our guide's flatbed Chevy was out of sight around the bend, but we could hear the thing grinding, rattling, and backfiring like a howitzer. Another few miles brought us to the lake.

Stu had never been here before, and Barragan told us that it was part of the Manitowish Waters Flowage. He backed his trailer down what passed for a boat launch and soon we were gliding across the still water to the far side. Cuno cut the motor and we coasted into a small bay surrounded with pines and leafless birch. Loons cried their lonesome call, the sound carrying and gathering intensity as it crossed the water: the signature of the North.

"Cast into shore along here," Barragan said, "We'll work the bays until the wind kicks up, then move to the windward shore. They like the broken water."

Stu began casting with a six-foot rod equipped with an Ambassador reel. The huge wooden plug arced through the air and landed with the delicacy of a rock. The rod bent some as he reeled the lure in.

I started casting my favorite pattern for musky and pike—a large red and white streamer weighted with heavy wire near the front. Barragan, still barefoot, watched us fish while sucking on a Kool and sipping coffee that had an unmistakable smell of bourbon to it. We cast for an hour without even a slight tug, then moved down to another bay.

About a dozen casts in, Stu's rod bent sharply and he hauled back on it, setting the hook with a series of vicious yanks. Something broke the surface 50 yards out and made a tremendous whoosh as it slammed back below the water. The drag hummed as the musky tore line from the reel, and the boat swung in the direction of the fish. The musky ran back and forth, never giving an inch. I was excited and offered suitable inanities along the lines of *keep the tip up*, *look at the size of that thing*, and the ever-popular *nice fish*. Barragan lit another smoke.

Ten minutes of fight and the fish began to yield to the pressure of the rod. Ten more minutes and it was thrashing beside the boat. Barragan netted the musky with a quick swoop and held it above the water. Big-headed. Wicked teeth. Coppery green with subtle vertical barring along the sides: a predator in appearance.

"Not bad, Stewart. Maybe 20 pounds, a little more. Want to kill it or let it go?"

"Turn it loose. We won't eat it and I'm not into wall mounts." Even when excited, Stu, like Barragan, played things close to the vest. That was just the way some people were. I, on the other hand, would have been hopping up and down and more than likely renewing my acquaintance with the water; that's just the way I am.

We fished for another couple of hours, and I managed to connect with a musky of 10 pounds. A small one, but a musky all the same. Some people have tried for years without any luck to take the species; but I'd been fortunate in catching a few dozen so far. The myth that muskies are hard to catch is just that—a myth. Find the fish and they will hit almost anything that comes their way, most of the time. They like big, deep water, and it takes years of exploration to nail down prime locations with any degree of consistency. Cuno knew the lakes and streams in the area better than anyone. He made good money as a guide and his taking us to this lake on his own time was a compliment to Stu. The effort indicated that Barragan considered my friend a good guy and not "an uppity pain in the ass from the city."

We broke for lunch after pulling in to shore and building a small fire.

"First fished here as a kid in the '20s. Dad was a gypo logger and was working some timber over that ridge. They camped along the shore and he always had a pole with him. First cast one night he caught a 30-pounder and a lot more after that," said Barragan. "Took me here and I did damn near the same. Bet I've fished the place 500 times. Ever tell you 'bout the big city fella and his lady that I brought here after the war? Almost got in trouble for that one.

"I'd been guiding this guy for about 10 years and he up and marries some rich girl from a suburb in Chicago. Lake

Forest or something. Calls and asks if I'd take the two of them fishing for a few days. They wanted, or at least he did, to catch some musky. The guy was all right and could fish a little, but he couldn't hold his liquor worth a tinker's damn. I said come up and so they did. Stayed at the Headwaters where I met them the next day. I'll leave their names out of it. They may still be alive and who knows who you two will talk to."

Barragan poured more coffee in his cup, then added a slash of Kessler's from a pint he pulled out of a pocket in his mackinaw. Stu produced a half-pint of his own from his tackle box and we each took a sip.

"Well, she was a looker for sure, and I always had a taste for the ladies, as you know. We loaded everything up in my old REO Speedwagon including the makings for a shore lunch. They always look forward to a big meal, and if I do things right, it's a dead bang guaranteed way to earn a fat tip, so I lay it on. Well, the mister brought a bottle of fancy Scotch and a couple bottles of French wine for the meal, and I figured 'What the hell. Things could get interesting here,' thinking all the time that he would get passed-out drunk and maybe I could lay a kiss on his lovely wife. You know what I mean," Cuno grinned as he worked over his coffee and torched a Kool. "I guess that was my plan, anyway. My brain didn't always do my thinking for me in those days.

"We piled into the truck and drove to where we put in today. For a couple of newlyweds, they didn't have much to say to each other. Things were pretty quiet while I got everything ready and put my 18-foot Voyager in the water. It was made of cedar stripping, wide, and stable. I figured we'd be okay. He sat up front with his cane rod, a real fancy one—a Payne I think. He had on one of those fancy Abercrombie & Fitch vests with so damn many pockets I don't know how he could find a thing in under an hour. A bunch of other useless duds, too. The Scotch went along up front with everything else. She sat in the middle, leaning back against a wooden rest I'd rigged up in the middle against a brace. The day was cloudy and a little on the chilly side, but at least there wasn't any wind. Not a bad day all-in-all for late September. We got to that bay back there and he started casting with some pretty salmon flies that I told him probably wouldn't work and were too nice to waste on the fish around here, anyway. He said they worked on Atlantic salmon in Norway and saw no reason why they wouldn't work in Wisconsin. It was his money, so I shut up.

"About every dozen casts he took a nip on the Scotch, and I figured a short day's fishing was staring him in the face. I pointed out the various ducks and birds to the lady and she got a kick out of watching the loons flying low across the water. She asked all sorts of questions about the types of trees and how old they were, how long geese lived and did they really mate for life. That kind of thing.

"Anyway, just when I figured we weren't going to do much in the way of fish if he kept using those flies of his, I'll be damned if a musky didn't slam one of his casts. There's a dumb fish in every lake, I suppose, and by the way his rod was bending and jerking around, it was a big one. Those old silk lines and gut leaders weren't made for sharp teeth, but he got lucky and the fish gave up in a hurry. I wanted to get one fish killed and in the boat for sure. My tip depended on it as much as that famous shore lunch. The musky was maybe three-and-one-half feet and close to 20 pounds. I popped it in the head with my .22 as it lay alongside us. It rolled in circles when I hit it, then died, and I grabbed the thing as quick as I could by the tail before it sunk to the bottom. I threw a loop of rope around it and we hauled it to shore.

"It was near lunch time as it was, and that lady was really worked up with the musky and the shooting and all. I don't think she'd ever seen doings like that back home. Her face was flushed and her breath came in short little gasps. Hell, that sound reminded me of something I'd had working in the back of my mind since I first saw her. The Scotch was in serious trouble up front and already he was feeling the booze. He almost fell in the lake trying to get out. I built a fire, which she loved, and they both tore into the lunch. The Scotch was more than half gone. He offered me some and I poured a couple of inches in my cup—good stuff. Beyond my budget. She worked on a bottle of that wine, and he took another slug of the Scotch, some of it running down his chin. Then he lay on his back and started snoring. That was my cue.

"I had some whiskey from a pint in my coat, then a little more. Then I moved next to her while I built up the fire. She was talking away a mile a minute about nothing that made any sense to me, and I opened another bottle of wine for her. She had a glow on to be sure. He seemed out cold and I sneaked a kiss. She liked that. I could tell and things moved awfully damn fast from there, though I had some trouble with the buttons on her pants. I'm not overly proud of what I did back then, but hell, I was young, in rut, and she was willing. Things happen. I guess.

"All of a sudden I saw him get up, grab my paddle, and smack me over the head. She rolled away and pulled her pants up, and he tripped over a rock and fell in the fire, rolling away and then lying on his back breathing hard, his coat smoking some.

"I got called all sorts of dirty names that I deserved, but he finally calmed down while I loaded up the gear. The fishing was over for that day and the rest of the trip. We paddled back without a word, a most uncomfortable feeling. She sat in the back of the truck and he was hunched over on the far side of the cab. No tip today, I figured. This was going to be a damned short marriage, but I was wrong on both counts. When we got back in town, he acted like nothing had happened, paid me in full, and gave me a $50 tip. Good money even today. I figured I'd keep my mouth shut for once in my life, and they left in a pricey Stutz Bearcat. Beautiful car. Beautiful woman. I heard that they're still married. Grandparents even. Hell of a way to kick off a life together, and I still hadn't learned my lesson, as I'm sure you've heard tell of Stewart."

"You're a real piece of work, Cuno. I'll give you that," said Stu as he puffed away on a Muriel. "How many times you been shot at going out a window of somebody's bedroom bare-assed naked? A hundred or so? The old man said you were a legend even in the '50s. How'd you get away with that crap?"

Barragan suggested that we work over where a coffee-colored stream poured in. The flow created gentle rips and chop for a hundred feet out into the lake. Stu stuck with his bomber plug. At Cuno's suggestion, I tied on two feet of 40-pound shock tippet to the 0X leader and switched from the red and white to a brown and gray streamer of gargantuan proportions. The entire monstrosity was about as long as one of my friend's hideous cigars. Cuno said that there were a "shit load" of rough fish holding in the creek at the mouth.

The streamer took some getting used to, but my old 9-weight Fenwick glass rod was up to the task. Primitive by today's way overpriced graphite items, but I've caught a "shit load" of fish on the thing and the rod is still with me. A small but pleasant connection with the past, I bring it out every year or so to fish for lake trout or pike. My pattern landed along the edge of the current just where the stream entered. I let it sink near the bottom and began to strip it toward the boat. Barragan said, "Heads up," and something ripped into the streamer that felt more like a Mack truck gone berserk than a fish. Line tore from my Pflueger (Yes, I still have this, too), and I was into the backing that was razoring through the calm surface of the lake many yards distant, cutting along the shoreline at an astounding clip.

"Reel in, damnit, Stewart," yelled Cuno as he fired up the motor and we were off in pursuit: a Chinese fire drill in the middle of the North Woods. Stu was laughing, smoking his 'gar and nipping at the pint with skilled synchronization. I took in line as fast as I could, but the hard-charging musky kept on going, never giving an inch.

Barragan shouted, "Damn crazy fish. He isn't even thinking of cover. He just wants to get the hell away from us." Barragan shouted. We'd covered hundreds of yards of shoreline and were running out of room. The fish was going to beach itself at this rate. Then it stopped and I frantically took up the slack. I pulled back on the musky and nothing happened. I might as well have been hooked to the bottom; the only difference being the palpable strumming of the line caused by the quivering of the fish's muscles holding it tight in the water. I was shaking. I knew this was a fish of a lifetime. We all did. Cuno edged the boat closer and I gained more line. Then we held this way in a standoff that lasted for what seemed like hours.

"Pull as hard as you can," Barragan said. "Don't jerk, just pull with all you've got. Stand up if you have to. I want to see this god-damned fish."

I did as I was told, but nothing happened, at first. Then, slowly, the musky came up, which felt like hauling a basketball up through a swimming pool filled with hardening cement. My arms ached. Then everything went nuts. The thing flew towards the surface at a slight angle away from us, then porpoised across the surface almost completely airborne.

"Jesus Christ," Stu screamed. "Look at that son-of-a-bitch. Forty pounds if it's a fucking inch."

The musky ran like a maniac perpendicular to us and Cuno followed. This went on for another 40 minutes. I feared for the health of the shock tippet as those teeth could certainly shred wire. The fish leaped again and I pulled back to keep the line tight. The musky stayed on the surface, swimming in wide circles.

"You've got a chance, John," whispered Barragan. Every sense I had was focused on that fish. I was more wired than I'd ever been; more than I ever would be again. Slowly, so damn slowly, the fish gave ground. Cuno stood, poised with the net. "Slowly. Slowly, John. Lead him here to me. He hasn't figured out the boat. One shot. Slowly. More. More. More...Got 'em," and Barragan snared the thing with a move so fast it would have put Michael Jordan to shame.

The musky was upset to some extent and thrashed and banged against the aluminum hull setting off a tremendous metallic racket that echoed back to us from the trees. Cuno pulled an old, green and silver scale from a pocket and hooked it to the net: 45 pounds.

"The net weighs a little less than six. You've got a 40-pounder here. Hell of a job on that outfit. Hell of a job on any outfit," and Cuno and Stu offered me their pints at once.

I put the rod down and took a slash off both of them, hands trembling badly. "Let him go, Cuno. That's too damn good a fish to kill." And he did with a quick twist of a pair of pliers and a swift turning of the net. The musky held for a second, then sank out of sight.

No one uttered a word. I turned to Cuno and his expression said it all. I'd passed his test and that made the day, one I'll never forget. School and college seemed worthless to me at the moment. All I really wanted to do was fish and hunt and hide out up here in the woods. Hell, shock treatments and massive doses of lithium couldn't shake the memory loose from my head.

When something works, you stick with it. With this salient thought firmly in mind, we found ourselves once more in Presque Isle at the Inn. The redoubtable Fabian manned the bar with skill and dispatch that were exemplary, even by the lofty standards established over the years in the North Woods. Beers and shots all around with gusto. I opted for a Point beer tonight. Pigs feet, Slim Jims, pretzels with French's mustard, and some stubby sausages skewered from a jar filled with a cloudy brine. Life was sweet tonight. George Jones was blathering away on the juke box, something about backing over his dog in the driveway and his wife leaving him for a septic tank disposal man. Life could be tough, too. We ate and drank and played some more pool, but opted for an early night after today's doings and the late night of before. Tomorrow Barragan was going to pick us up at our place for a day of killing—grouse, woodcock, a white-tail buck (yes, we had our tags and plenty of blaze orange), and some walleyes that we would fillet and grill for dinner back at the peninsula. Stu built a roaring fire, and we smoked a couple of White Owls before going on the nod. They really were awful cigars.

The next morning Stu was all worked up about something, pacing back and forth in the kitchen and muttering, "She's here again. She's back. I knew she wouldn't let me down."

"What the hell, Stu? Now what?"

"The ghost. The one that lived here before we bought the land. She died in a fire 60 years ago. I see her all the time. There's lipstick on my coffee cup. Look."

I did and didn't see anything, but I've found it is best to humor Stu at times like these. "You gone over on me. Let me look at your lips, sweetie." No lipstick, but you never knew what he was up to half the time. Later on down the road he killed himself, despondent that someone had stolen one of his inventions involving cold temperatures and electrical conductivity. Too smart and too damn sensitive for his own good, but that sad fate was way off in the distance, not yet realized. "Okay. So there's a ghost. You have lunch and coffee made for today? How 'bout the beer and a little something stronger. We can't let Cuno down."

"It's all taken care of, in the cooler on the landing," said Stu while touching off a Muriel the size of a cheap ballpark hotdog. Clouds of off-colored smoke, blue and black like bad exhaust from a Caterpillar D9 rose to the ceiling. "Maybe she'll be here when we get back."

"She have a friend?"

"Screw off, Holt."

Some minutes later as the day turned light out, the sound of Barragan's "Indian Wagon" (his name) vibrated through the pines, the coughs, sputters, and piercing backfires heralding his approach and, more than likely, stampeding all the game for miles around. We grabbed orange coats and hats, rifles, shotguns, fishing equipment, a cooler, thermos jugs, beer, and cigars: a Spartan expedition if ever I saw one. We loaded all of this stuff in back on the staked bed of Cuno's truck. His Brittany, Maggie, was running from side to side, eager to chase some birds. We piled in the cab and thundered down the road: mayhem on the loose; lunatics escaped; mental deficients with no redeeming value, wildly out of control. Another normal day for some of us. May it always be so.

Cuno drove for miles along narrow logging roads that ran between dense stands of pines and birch, just barely above the water line of large marshes. Herons, crows, chickadees, and an osprey were sighted. Abruptly, he pulled over beside a stand of birch that grew on the side of a long, gentle rise. We grabbed our guns and Cuno turned the dog loose. We fanned out and side-hilled our way not far above the road. Maggie worked in close and only needed an occasional voice correction. We kicked up grouse steadily and soon had our limit. The leaves were gone. The dog worked like a champ and for some reason all three of us shot well. Stu doubled on the first flush. Dropping down, we crossed the road and hunted back to the rig. More grouse that we passed on and then a pair of wood-cock. I dropped one that juked left and Barragan and Stu drilled the other. Not much to retrieve there, but Cuno knew where the birds were, that was clear.

"My best cover over here. Never failed to kick up a bunch with Maggie along," said Cuno. "There's better habitat east of Boulder, but this is on the way to the lake we're going to fish. And I spotted a good buck in a tight draw nearby. If we set up right and Stewart doesn't poison the air with those cheap-ass cigars of his, we'll get him. He always works his way down to the lake around dusk. I've been saving him for a client, but you two will do."

Barragan didn't have his boat with him, but he said he had a canoe stashed at the lake. No flyfishing today. Walleyes will take things like jigs and Rapalas on ultra-light tackle, which is nice sport, but flyfishing is mostly futile unless you're working moving water with heavily-weighted streamers. We'd go the bait route today, using minnows and sinkers that looked like diminutive doorknobs. Lord forgive us all.

We paddled out to a small, rocky island, rigged up, and dropped our offerings out into the lake. According to Cuno, there was a submerged ridge that held baitfish and walleyes up to 10 pounds. The lake was medium-sized with no cabins as it was too far out in the boonies and too swampy and buggy during prime tourist season to receive much attention. We fished from about 10:30 until two and caught more than enough for dinner. The walleye took softly, playing with the bait before chomping on the minnows. That's when we set the hook. They were strong but not much in the way of fighters. Two were in the five-pound range, and the rest were from one to three pounds. Two-thirds of our work was completed; time for a leisurely lunch, a quick nap by the fire and then off to whitetailville.

Later, we drove another mile or so on what could be called a road if a person was feeling generous. We stopped and Stu grabbed his 25/06. One rifle was plenty, and anyway, it was his turn; I'd nailed the musky yesterday and Barragan had already filled his tags. We walked along the overgrown lane for another mile, then pushed up a small cut in the land that had a tiny trickle of water. We found some cover behind a patch of blueberry bushes and waited quietly. The day began to dim towards night. Not even the sound of birds. A cool breeze drifted down the draw. I thought we were out of luck with the buck and was ready to say so, when I saw my friend slowly raise his gun and fire. The sound was like a bomb dropped in the middle of this silence. The rich smell of gunpowder filled the air.

I never saw the deer, but Stu and Barragan did see it fall 50 yards away. A clean heart shot. Eight points. Fat. A healthy deer. Stu unsheathed his knife, rolled up his sleeves and bled the animal, cutting with practiced strokes. Efficient. Workmanlike. He placed the liver in a plastic bag Cuno handed him. Blood was streaked on his arms up to his elbows and covered his hands. We dragged the buck to the road, which wasn't hard work among the three of us. We hefted the carcass into the back, let Maggie out of the cab, and roared back to the cabin, the three of us swilling our first beers of the day and nipping on the whiskey. Cigars and cigarettes were in order, and with them the cab clouded up with acrid smoke.

"Jesus. I can't breath," coughed Stu.

Cuno started rolling down his window but Stu said in protest, "Barragan, don't wreck the damn ambiance we got going here. People pay good money for this sort of thing."

"If you say so Stewart."

Back at camp, Stu built a fire and torched the coals in the Weber, then went out to help Cuno hang the deer. Maggie followed me around, and I filled a bowl with water and another with Purina. She'd earned her supper tonight. I filleted the fish, wrapped bakers in foil with sliced onions, and built a salad. I swiped a bottle of passable white wine that I discovered in one of the cabinets, and set the table. While the potatoes were cooking, we sat in front of the crackling blaze of birch nursing our drinks and reliving the day. Barragan said that this was the kind of trip he liked best, the kind where he didn't have to babysit some idiots from the city. A day where he got to shoot and fish. He'd spent his entire life living this way and couldn't imagine doing things any other way. Stu cooked the fillets to perfection, and with a squeeze of lemon they were superb. We ate like slobs and Stu's father's wine supply suffered serious damage. There was some more talk after dinner, including a brief bit of jive about Stu's ghostly lady. She stood us up and we were disappointed. Oh well, can't have everything, I guess.

Sometime near midnight, Cuno left for home. He was a good man. I was lucky to have spent this time with him and luckier still when I had several opportunities to hunt and fish with him in the coming years.

Sadly, both my friends are dead now, way too soon. But we couldn't complain. One way or the other, we'd done our share of damage, had our share of good times and laughs. But still, I wish the three of us could have gotten together in Montana to raise some serious hell in the mountains and on the high plains.

Maybe next time around.

F·I·V·E

A Woman Castoff

NERVOUSNESS AND FLYFISHING normally don't go together when I'm out on the water. The idea, at least as I see things, is to soak in the surroundings, appreciate the river, catch a fish or two, and "thank the day" (as musician Ben Sidran used to say). And I could care less what others, including guides, think of my casting technique, the quality of the flies I tie, or the way I play a trout. Life is too short to be concerned with opinions regarding these relatively unimportant aspects of existence. So when I found myself in a state of high self-consciousness, I became alarmed. What was going on? Had I lost what remained of my mind? Had I tripped over that fearful edge that defined the boundary between reality and yuppydom? Was I starting to fish for all the wrong reasons?

No, not really; at least not today. The reason for my unusual emotional state was quite simple: I was fishing with a woman guide. One who was funny, intelligent, nice looking, and a hell of a lot better angler than I was. This was an uncommon situation, actually a first for me, but I was dealing with it with a grace and panache more commonly associated with former Cleveland Indians' slugger Albert Bell when anyone had the temerity to ask him for an autograph—in other words, not well. My palms were damp, and perspiration was

81

beading on my forehead despite the fact that there was still snow on the ground on this pleasant April day. This was awful beyond belief. I'd terrified, scared off, or put down dozens of large cutthroat, browns, and brook trout. My flies were tangled, while tippets were busted and snarled in astonishing profusion among the bushes along the creek. Line was curled around my feet, legs, and arms, and that was after what qualified as a decent cast for me this afternoon.

Yes, I'd made a fool of myself around women before, made a sad career of it in fact. But never on a trout stream. I'd been casting for over 30 years. Flyfishing was second nature. I could, and have, dropped a fly where I wanted it while unconscious. But not this time out. Happily, as I said before, my companion possessed a wonderful sense of humor.

Jamie Phelan laughed at the confusion I was experiencing; not necessarily at me, but at the absurdity of a grown man being reduced to complete and total uncoordinated chaos simply by her presence. She'd been on this trip before—many times. Had seen male egos die a humiliating death on a trout stream, and she was not the least bit vindictive or gleeful with our obvious discomfort. She understood and worked like a joyful demon to relieve the tension, to make things better, to point out the happy lunacy of the situation. She was an artful magician, but I was a tough case. However, like any good woman, she was determined in her own cheerful way. I'd catch a trout and have fun doing it even if she died laughing in the process. I was a brave soul out here in this high altitude, wide-open, Wyoming mountain valley.

Jamie said she was going downstream to look for some working fish and suggested that I move up around the bend (been there, done that before) and cast to some large cutthroat that might be feeding on small mayflies. I could hear her gentle chuckle as she headed off. Her departure might well come under the heading of a mercy disappearance. I silently thanked Jamie for her thoughtfulness and moved 100 yards up the creek. Several very big cutthroat, over two feet, were leisurely sipping baetis in the smooth water. Many other trout were visible holding on the bottom. The water was so clear, I felt like I was looking through pure air at the fish as they held in the easy current with the slightest of flicks by their tails.

I was amazed at how quickly my casting returned to the lofty level of expertise that I was used to. Alone without the mirthful Jamie grinning at my shoulder, I regained a semblance of confidence. Crouching next to a small alder I cast about 30 feet with a slight mend. The fly landed well above a steadily feeding cutthroat, drifted drag-free, and then I saw open jaws, showing white against the dark of the streambed silt. A large swirl from the nonchalant take. I set the hook and the trout immediately pulled hard for some cover across the creek, moving with power and speed and aided by the current. I managed to check the fish that then ran back and forth boiling the surface. Other trout followed it on either side, curious, no doubt, about their brother's strange behavior. The fish tired in a hurry, and I pulled it to the grassy bank and scooped my net under it—well over 20 inches. Dark shaded with deep blues, reds, and oranges. Flaming cuts on the jaw. Ink-black spotting with a patina of silver accenting the color scheme. A beautiful representative of its species. I hated to release the trout, but I did, and watched as it swam off and immediately returned to its holding water.

"Nice job, John. Let's see if you can do it with a real woman watching," and her laughter bounced around in the early spring sunshine. I never heard her approach. A dangerous woman, this one. "Come on, show me what you got, big boy. Take your best shot."

The obvious double entendre broke me up, and I began to relax and asked her if she was sure she could handle my presentation.

"I'll do my best. Been looking forward to some action all afternoon, John. Let 'er rip."

Flyfishing sure has changed in a hurry over the last few years, I thought. I was beginning to believe that this was all for the better. When I rationally examined the deal, I had to admit that spending an afternoon with an attractive female offered a bit more intrigue and aesthetic enhancement than killing time with one of my hardcore male fishing buddies.

This particular afternoon actually took place a number of years ago, and I am reliving the proceedings from the safe distance of time passed. Since then I've become good friends with Jamie, gotten to know her well—her joys, likes, dislikes, triumphs, sorrows, and her unique way of living a life that few of us can imagine. Jamie's really one of a kind, not an ersatz amalgam of plastic images shabbily constructed for the insecure purposes of titillation or individuality—whatever that may be. My first inkling that this person was more than she seemed came on that first day together. After we were done fishing and removing our waders back at her pickup, she pulled off her heavy sweater, and the top to her silk long underwear rose above her midriff revealing a tattoo that said *Hurt In Love* done in Helvetica style lettering.

"Jamie, I must ask. What's with the tattoo?"

"I like to read. A falconer friend of mine does, too. He turned me on to William T. Vollmann, lots of his books like *The Rainbow Stories.* In one of them, *The Happy Girls*, a Thai prostitute has a tattoo on her ass that says the same thing. It applies to me in two obvious ways that I'm sure you can guess and one other that would surprise you, to say the least."

"How so?"

"You don't know me well enough for that one, John my boy."

"Come on, Jamie. Give me a break."

"Maybe next time, dear. Have some wine," and she handed me a glass of Soave that glowed subtly golden in a longstemmed crystal glass. Yes, Crystal. Strange days one more time.

We finished off the day with a few drinks and about 85 pounds of ribs each at a nice joint down the road. I had to fly home the next morning—Jackson to Stapleton to Salt Lake to Kalispell: the old "you can't get there from here" syndrome. Jamie had friends north of Whitefish who she planned to visit in late August, so we made casual arrangements to fish the Blackfeet Reservation for a day or two later that summer.

The months passed along as they usually do, with some writing, a lot of fishing, hours of nothing but sitting in the sun, and other energetic activities, and soon it was closing in on September when the phone rang. Sometimes I can tell by the ring who is on the other end, like I did then.

"John. It's Jamie. I just bought three days of permits for the Res down at Lakestream (the local fly shop owned by friends of mine). Let's head over tomorrow. Are you game?"

"Of course. Where are you?" and she told me, and next morning she bounced out of the front door of her friends' home down by the train depot. She was loaded down with rods, waders, a duffel bag, and a cooler. We dumped the stuff in the back of the truck and headed east over the mountains, along the Middle Fork of the Flathead, and past the southern edge of Glacier Park. A beautiful day. Cloudless. Warm. Goats worked a salt lick near Marias Pass and Jamie made me stop for photographs. The river flowed emerald blue far below us. The first hint of autumn colors to come flickered in an easy breeze.

"Windy times on the Res," I thought, where a calm day was when things were in the 30 mph range. I'd been there when they were in the 80 mph range, and it was absolutely unfishable. But I've always taken conditions as they come: fish when the elements let you. I'd made reservations at Jacobson's for one of their cabins in East Glacier. There were several decent restaurants in the area, and plus, I'd packed a small Weber to grill steaks. We'd survive if not actually flourish. It would all work out, one way or the other. The Res is out-of-this-world fishing and is fun even when the trout (mainly rainbows and browns of enormous size at times) fail to cooperate. The juxtaposition of wide-open prairie abutting raging mountains is surreal, disorientating. I love it and was sure Jamie would, too.

Jamie reached in the cooler and pulled out a pair of brown bottles: Montana nut brown ale brewed by another friend (I still had a few) in Whitefish. Rich brown foam bubbled from the mouths when the caps were pried off. "Excellent, don't you think?" said Jamie, draining hers in one take. "I hear you know the guy who brews this."

"You might say that. We've shared a time or two together." Friend or not, Gary does make the best beer I've ever tasted, but I've always kept looking just to keep him on his toes.

"Never can have too many brewmeisters on your side, I always say."

"I bet you do, Jamie. Let's get going. I doubt we can cheat the wind, but we can try. We'll dump our gear and head off to Goose Lake. Some browns might be working in a bay I know there."

We thundered off down the road with all four cylinders of the truck roaring in powerful precision. All 36 horses pulling together as one. The scenery shifted from alpine to scrub pine and aspen, then broke loose into the vast expanse of the high plains. You could lose your mind out here, and some of us have, more than once.

After checking in, we bounded down Highway 49, then 89. An excellent drive along the eastern edge of Glacier that winds through groves of aspen and stands of pine dwarfed from the constant poundings of a relentless wind that wails along the Rocky Mountain Front. Views that stretched for mad miles up ice-carved valleys that dead-ended when they crashed against shear walls of granite and limestone, which rose for many feet and were covered with snow and retreating ice fields. Finger-like lakes that resembled fjords filled the narrow valleys. Small streams that protected sometimes not-so-small trout glistened beneath the sun as the water slid through dense tangles of alder. Tough, almost impossible to fish, but still worth a try on days of rare courage and strained judgment.

"You sure picked a poor place to call home, John," Jamie said as she leaned through the cab's sliding back window mining for ale. "I may have to move up here. The skiing isn't as good as Jackson, but I'm used to hard times. And I've got you to call and rile up. Yep. Northwest Montana is starting to look pretty damn appealing to this girl. How come there aren't more people?"

"Lot's of summer homes, but most of the rich transients don't like the snow and the cold, thank God. What we really need is a strain of ebola that attacks developers and realtors who are only in it for a buck. I hate the bastards."

"Calm down. None of that save-the-Earth silliness on this trip. We're here to catch fish! Damn big ones. Time to raise a little hell with the trouts. You look like you could use a long run. Blow off some steam. I'm just the woman for the job."

"Don't break your arm, there, Jamie," and I worked on the beer as the foam dripped onto my lap.

"Can't take some people anywhere. Your mother must be sick at how you turned out. I'm sure she had high expectations. And look at you. Divorced. A house full of dogs, cats, guns, and fly rods. And a writer to boot. She must be just sick."

"Thanks. I'll take you over to her place to meet her. You can tackle one of her punch bowl-sized Old Fashioneds."

Talking, listening to Little Elmo and the Iguana Kings on the tape, and taking in the mind-blowing scenery, it would be easy to forget about fishing on a cruise like this one, but we made it to Goose, eventually, and soon found ourselves lurching and bouncing along muddy, rutted cow trails that doubled as roads on the Reservation. To make things interesting, there were often large rocks hiding beneath the brown puddles. My muffler had not experienced an easy life. The truck was hardly Rolls-Royce quiet.

White-capped waves pounded the shore. Spray whipped off to the east driven by the wind. The breakers were only three feet high or so. Fishable and the big trout loved to hang near the crests drinking in the oxygen. Sight fishing for torpedoes in the surf during a mini-hurricane. I loved this, too, and I was sure that Jamie would, also.

We parked at the bay I'd mentioned, rigged up with 8-weights for the wind, hoped for some big trout, and plunged into the water. The waves rocked both of us with each surge, but in minutes we'd grown accustomed to their pace and the wavering motion was not a problem. Jamie moved out, off to my right to take advantage of the wind. Few people look good in neoprene waders. I sure don't. And to prove it, a friend sent me some dupes of slides he'd taken of me on a chaotic trip to Iceland one year: blackmail in its lowest form.

Not so with Jamie. She was tall with a trim athletic body. The waders did little to detract from her appearance. I watched as she punched her line cross-wind with an effortless double-haul. Big, almost masculine hands working together with well-practiced grace. Her long, curly-brown hair fully extended in the gale. A much fairer sight than those presented by companions of mine from, say, Boston or Baton Rouge or Frisco, Colorado.

The sun illuminated the waves. They practically fluoresced an intense sapphire. Large shapes, trout, were visible riding along the tops and holding the troughs. Jamie launched a cast that landed ahead of a fish, then twitched and stripped a #2 black bugger with feminine enticement. I saw the trout turn and slam the streamer. No delicate set here. She reefed back on the rod, bending backwards at an obvious angle. The fish exploded straight out of the wave and knifed into another several feet away. Silvery with hints of brown and yellow and black spots, and I even saw the kype and the bugger hooked in the upper corner of the jaw. The fish race-horsed through the water and air, crashing in fountains of spray as it ran along the bottom for yards, tearing backing from the reel.

Trout on the Res often pass the 10-pound mark. The water is fertile, to state things mildly, and the browns and rainbows grow fast, strong, and large. This fish of Jamie's was in that category. With 2X tippet, she'd win the fight as long as the leader didn't fray from the trout's teeth. More wave diving and mad, submerged dashes before tiring. She slowly brought the brown to her, then quickly grabbed it by the tail and dropped her rod to hold the fish—easily 10 pounds.

"Not bad for a rookie, girl." I hollered, "There's hope."

Grinning. Glowing. Her face was flushed with the rush of the struggle. Behind her, a nice picture with the solitary peak of Chief Mountain showing purple, gray, and pink. The brown swam off slowly upon release and Jamie started casting again. She hadn't uttered a word but the expression on her face said it all. The Res had hooked another one.

I could see that the next few days were not going to offer much in the way of sleep. I like to fish with those who go all day and most of the night. Hell, we can catch up on nap time when we get home. Burn the candle at both ends. Blow up all the bridges.

"Your turn John, dear," she shouted above the wind.

"Jamie, you're the second woman this year to call me dear. And the first one damn near drove me insane."

"Don't call me a woman. A lady, yes, but never a woman," and she howled in a strange way, made more so by the wind that twisted and bent the untamed sound: not like a wolf; not like a human; not like anything I'd ever heard. Plain crazy along the Front.

The "trouts," as Jamie put it, were active throughout the afternoon, and we took our share. Mostly browns along with a couple of rainbows thrown in. That's how the fishing can be over here: steady with an average of five pounds or more. Then there are days when nothing happens and you can't blame it on the wind. In fact, the few calm days I've experienced over here haven't been worth the effort—one or two fish or none. The flat conditions make the fish spooky, secretive. Wind drives oxygen into the water, breaks up the surface, and makes the trout aggressive. But by five the typhoon was in full force, and casting with any degree of accuracy, distance, and safety was long gone. We decided to drive back by way of Browning, the largest town in Blackfeet country. Rolling hills, coulees, and bluffs drifted off for miles in every direction, all colored yellow brown by native grasses and harvested crops. In the spring, the place was brilliant emerald with wildflowers sprinkled about—azure, crimson, orange, yellow, white, pink. Cattle fed with languid intensity on the stubble. Groups of horses stood with studied boredom, their rumps to the wind, tails blown between their legs. We didn't see any game—no deer, antelope, elk, or upland birds. Most of the animals were in hiding; open season was always on at the Res. Make an appearance and you were dinner. Isolated farms were tucked away from the road along brushy streams. Rusting farm machinery and cars up on blocks seemed to be in every yard. Jamie shoved a tape of the Cranberries in the machine. A strange group wailing eerily with Celtic-tribal overtones, which was more than appropriate for this journey.

Talk turned to books for some reason. I was nearly sick of talking about books and writing. Most of the time I enjoy talking about writing, but I'd just finished a batch of magazine articles and a book revision. I'd had enough. Life is tough.

Jamie rambled on about Vollmann again, his trips to Afghanistan, Somalia, and scariest of all, darkest LA where he'd hung out with hookers afflicted with AIDS. She wandered through the likes of Chatham, Bodio, Jones, Proulx, Middleton, and Traver. She was well-read when it came to fishing, hunting, and other atrocities. I began to feel faint. Then she turned on me, and sensing the approaching ugliness, I requested a beer and was promptly handed another foaming bottle.

"I've read some of your stuff. I liked the bit about you screwing the girl every time you shot a grouse, and *Chasing Fish Tales* had its moments, but a lot of it was crapola. I couldn't figure it out at first, then it dawned on me that you like to write about garbage. You're a dumpster poet in a low-level way. Ever think about writing a book that was good all the way through?"

"Thanks. I hope you know you're paying for the room and our meals."

"No really. Why do you write about all that environmental bull and what flies to use? Who cares, anyway?"

"It takes up space. Not as much of my mind works as well as it should or used to, okay?"

"Sometime you should come right out and tell the readers that you're talking to them and you want to hear from them. Establish a dialogue."

"Oh, Jesus. Jamie, I'm only in it for the little money I make. As long as they pay for the books and the royalty checks don't bounce, I could care less. Look at all the junk written about flyfishing and bird hunting. Hundreds of books a year about the same thing. I'm no better than the rest of the hacks, and I stopped caring a million words ago. It's awful. It's painful to read some of it. In 10 years maybe one book in a hundred will be remembered and mine won't be among them. I'll probably be dead anyway."

"You're selling yourself short, John."

"You got the selling part right, but you're confusing self-deprecation with realism."

Thankfully, Browning came into view and the subject finally died a merciful death. I like the Blackfeet people. A good friend of mine, a fishing and bird hunting buddy, is a tribal member, but Browning depressed me, especially in the dead of winter when a cruel wind howled so incessantly, and snow drifted against the curbs and dilapidated buildings. People freeze to death and no one cares. There are suicides, murders, and other forms of recreation bred by frustration. Poverty and alcoholism is rampant, and despite the concerted efforts of the tribe to improve the lot of its people, progress is achingly slow. The good life is a very long way off for many of them here.

Because tourist season was still flaming away in mindless idiocy, the town was bustling. Out-of-state plates from Alberta, New Jersey, Illinois, Texas, and parts beyond far outnumbered state licenses. Groups of Indians, beaten down from a life of failure and heavy drinking, stood around passing bottles in paper bags back and forth and smoking cigarettes. They eyed the traffic with weary anger. Jamie was fascinated by the scene, but I was glad when we hit the highway heading west to the mountains and our cabin. Time to clean up, have a relaxed drink, watch the evening news, and go out for dinner. Seeing the men in town made me feel guilty at my easy trip, one filled with friends and high times chasing birds and fish. I didn't dwell on this, but instead concentrated on the wild mountains dominating the horizon and the rafts of clouds that clung to the peaks.

The Summit House is a restaurant on the Blackfeet Reservation, perched on a pine-shrouded knoll that gives way to an impressive view of the overthrust of Little Dog and Beaverhead Mountain. These peaks, rising 4,000 to almost 9,000 feet above us, consist of Precambrian rock over a billion years old that slid for 35 miles over infant Cretaceous formations of only 65 million years. The forces involved go way beyond my comprehension. Even today, Chief Mountain occasionally experiences shifts, or prolonged mini-earthquakes, that "liquefy" its rock and cause dangerous slides and tremors. In the dark shales, ammonites, close relatives of the modern-day pearly nautilus, are present. Looking like large snails, they are actually closer to an octopus that hangs out in a shell. Pine, larch, and aspen forest rolls off and climbs to the treeline not far above the high valley. A small creek dotted with beaver ponds glistened in the dying colors of sunset. Stars turned on above the mountains—not a bad view from our table located next to a huge window. A few more places like this and the Blackfeet would be in business. We ordered drinks, the house salad, ribeyes, and a bottle of Merlot for the meal.

"Yah, Holt. I'm moving up here. The place never quits, does it?" Jamie's eyes were glowing, shooting sparks as she took in the scene. A few deer made a cocktail-hour appearance 50 yards away, grazing leisurely as they drifted across a tall grass meadow. "Life's too damn short to waste this country."

We sipped our drinks and stared into space, something I was a past-master at and had been for decades. Jamie was pretty good at the pursuit, herself. Salads and more drinks arrived in artful precision and were dispatched promptly. Then the steaks, done up rare, and the dry wine and some sautéed mushrooms. All were gone in an instant. Cognac and black coffee. We were feeling okay. Enjoying the easy side of a fine day.

"Jamie, how in the hell did you ever turn to guiding? I can't see you putting up with the bozos, all the clowns who surely must eye you with lecherous intent."

"You mean the way you look at me, bad boy? No, I like being on the river and fishing. The chance to meet people and spin the random idiot's head around is worth the bullshit. It's a challenge. The pay is okay, and if I shimmy a little during the float, the tips ain't bad either. I could never hack a nine-to-five gig with some jerk telling me what to do all day long. I enjoy teaching people things about flyfishing and about the land. Watching someone catch their first cutthroat is a gas, one I never tire of. And I just like being on rivers, experiencing their personalities. If only more people were like a classy trout stream. A better world for you and me, John. Wouldn't that be wonderful? Mister Roger's neighborhood and all that saccharine silliness. This country still blows my mind. We're stunned at wackos like Manson and Richard Speck. Evil dudes that off a dozen people each, yet we actually allow a convicted felon like Ollie North to run for Senate. Or we let G. Gordon Liddy out in public. A strange society we got going here. Oh well, at least they haven't locked you and me up. Yet.

"I've been doing this, working through other outfitters mostly, for 13 years. Ever since I came back from Denmark. I lived in Copenhagen for almost two years. It took me that long to grow accustomed to the place, the culture, and the changes I was going through. But finally I headed back to the States and the West where my heart will always be."

"What did you do over there for all that time?" I asked.

"Drank their excellent beer and smoked their excellent hash. Partied. I was a bad girl. And over the course of events, I changed my way of life, as they say."

"In what way? You don't impress me as a person enamored with self-help jive or classical philosophical examinations. More a Bill Burroughs type of guy."

"You're closer than you think," and she drained her drink and asked for another round. "You'll figure all this out someday. This is a neat guessing game, don't you think?"

"I hate games, Jamie."

"You'll learn to love this one, John dear."

That damn "dear" stuff again. We finished off our brandies in silence, grooving on the icebergs as an old friend used to say years ago. Then we headed out into the cool night. There was so much starlight there were shadows cast by the building, the trees. To the truck and an easy cruise home. Jamie wanted to watch Australian Rules football on ESPN. God! Another late night to make my morning sport painful. So what? I was having fun. We killed a few more hours laughing at the ridiculous game and talking about sports. Who the hell is Vic Davalilo, anyway? Not the one on the Bitterroot. This boy played for the Indians a long time ago, about the same period as the skillful Andre "he-boots-it" Rodgers did for the Cubs. I would have enjoyed hearing a tape of our conversation.

The next day we hit another lake, this one jammed up against the mountains. The wind blew in spates of violence, but there were periods of relative calm where we could climb in our float tubes and work the rainbows that rose to crane-flies and hoppers and Callibaetis mayflies and sometimes a damsel fly nymph a few feet beneath the surface. The fish were from two to seven pounds: long runners, tough fighters, but not much in the way of acrobatics. All the same, we enjoyed ourselves before heading into town for Mexican food and margaritas, then more talk back at the room with the intellectual stimulation of MTV in the background.

Our last day we drove east to Four Horns, a large lake way out on the plains. A creek comes in on one end, and often, large browns and rainbows congregate there. You have to wade through sticky muck and soupy cow pies to get to the best spot, but that's all part of the charm. Two ponds above the lake sometimes hold huge fish, to 17 pounds based on photos I've seen, but they were devoid of trout that day. The little creek that connects the ponds and lakes also holds fish, and we caught a couple of one-pound rainbows on hoppers. We worked the outlet with olive woolly buggers, and the fishing was steady for fat rainbows.

We were so keyed into the fishing that we scarcely noticed the dark clouds rolling in low and angry. By chance I looked up and saw the ones above us boiling and whirling like vertical tornadoes. The truck was a mile away, and this crud looked like heavy rain, hail, lots of wind, and there was already lightning grounding on the far shore: wicked, jagged bolts slamming the earth. The faint scent of ozone reached me.

"Jamie, let's get the hell back to the truck," I said, but she was already way ahead of me, high-stepping as best she could through the mud. We made the far shore, getting covered in the slop in the process, when the brunt of the weather hit. There was a slight bank of four or five feet that offered a modicum of shelter and we took it thankfully. Rain came down so thickly you could not see the lake 20 feet away. Wind was screaming, howling as it tore across the open landscape, through the tall grass. Lightning slashed across the sky with thundering explosions almost at the same time. My ears hurt. The ground shuddered. Jamie grinned in a gallows humor sort of way, and we held on to each other. There was so much electricity in the air, the hair on my arms and on her neck was standing up. Oh shit. We're dead, I thought. The monster raged over us for 20 of the longest minutes of my life. Forever. Then the storm quit but decided to toss some hail in our direction for good measure. Large stuff, about the size of British golf balls. This didn't last long, but I caught one in the cheek that smarted a bit. Then the storm moved off toward Cut Bank. The sun came out and a rainbow arced from one side of Four Horns to the other.

"Sure beats drugs, but I could go for a beer and a cigar," Jamie said standing up and shaking some of the rain off her. The ground was littered with hail. The place looked like a Shriner benefit golf tournament run amuck. Going back to the truck was like walking on ball bearings.

An eventful and enjoyable three days on the Res, then a couple more spent knocking around Whitefish, fishing some rivers and mountain streams, a bit of carousing in the evenings (including taking in Norton Buffalo and the boys in concert at The Glacier Grande). Unique harmonica riffs on a warm, late-summer night. Jamie was right, life IS tough up here. Maybe

I'll move back to Beloit, Wisconsin, and get a job on the assembly line.

The year passed with both of us doing our normal, irresponsible things, with only a few letters and phone calls between us. Then in late August she called and said she was packing up a U-Haul to move to Whitefish and would I help drive the truck? I figured it would be a treat, so I bought a ticket (money to burn) and did the reverse hop from Kalispell to Jackson. The last leg on a MetroLiner was choppy at best, but I made it in three bounces. Jamie was there with the U-Haul and her 1972 Toyota Landcruiser in tow.

"Ready to go? I figure we can make West Yellowstone in three hours easy," and she grabbed my duffel. "I'm payin' for the ride. You do the driving. I hate this big piece of junk. We can fish the Gallatin and the Jefferson and that little stream over by Helena you're always babbling about."

The show must and did go on. We gleefully drove across Grand Teton National Park passing through a blizzard hatch of RVs spewing aromatic clouds of partially burned hydrocarbons. And the beat went on as we zipped into Yellowstone at upwards of 11 miles-per-hour, winding up at Old Faithful six years later. We set our sights on scenic downtown West Yellowstone, and in what seemed like mere weeks, pulled into some God-forsaken motel where Jamie had made reservations. Dinner was hastily consumed amid tables full of cheery visitors wearing cheap felt hats festooned with fluffy pink feathers and poor-fitting T-shirts that did little to disguise their large beer bellies, and most of these were worn by women and young children. Phrases like "The Blue Goose Lives" or "Mammoth Hot Springs Ain't The Only Big Thing Around Here" were silk-screened in sedate shades of chartreuse and flaming pink across these shirts. I was terrified. This was the type of crowd that could turn on the unwary in an instant, devouring my frail body with loud crunchings of bone and toothsome rippings of flesh. I wanted out, but Jamie was beside herself with joy, laughing freely and carrying on incoherent conversations with the beasts occupying adjacent tables. But I couldn't handle this anymore and made a quick exit, bumping into chairs, the checkout stand, and nearly walking through the glass of the exit door.

The next day we fished both the Gallatin (for a few tired rainbows) and the Jefferson near dusk for several big browns. We had another appointment with modern mediocrity in the form of a bomb shelter masquerading as a motel in Helena. Jamie sure knew how to travel.

Thankfully, we made it over MacDonald Pass next morning and were soon working our way upstream casting elk hair caddis and hopper imitations tight beneath overhanging willows and alders. This time of year the fish only run between 9 and 17 inches, but they were strong, beautiful fish, and any decent cast and drift translated into a brown.

We stopped at a large pool guarded by a willow leaning out over the stream. A number of browns were sipping the gray caddis that were coming off or hammering grasshoppers that landed on the water through random errors in judgment. We sat on a log and watched the spectacle. The fish rose steadily, making circles that broke up as they drifted away with the current.

"Ever hear of a band called the Finchley Boys, John?"

In fact I had, but that was really a long time ago.

"I guess you would have, being from the Midwest back then. Remember the singer? Long red-brown hair and frilly shirts. He looked like a woman. And he always had that boa constrictor draped around his shoulders. That whole visual confused the hell out of me. Took me a long time to even accept how weird they were, or how strange I was, for that matter."

"I remember the guy and that goofy bass player with the curly hair that grew down his face. He'd cut holes in it by his eyes and paint blue glass frames on. What a crew." How could I forget that blitzed-out day at Lake Forest College. Lord knows I've tried.

"They could really rip when they wanted to," said Jamie.

"They played music, too? What brought this topic up, anyway?"

"I don't know, maybe just the notion of fooling a living thing with a fake, a fly that passes for the real article even though it's something else. Idle musings, nothing more."

We finished the last stretch of good water, walked down a dirt road that led back to the truck and motored off toward home, which we made in three hours. Jamie spent the next week moving her stuff into a small cabin she'd rented outside of town. I was busy doing nothing and did not see her again until she pulled in front of the house a week later.

"Found a job, sort of. Actually two jobs," she said while opening each of us a nut brown ale plucked from a front-seat cooler. "I'm doing a little guiding and giving casting lessons a couple of times a week in the evening. And come ski season, I'll be working at the Hibernation House up on The Mountain during the day at the front desk. Looks like I'm in your back-yard for the duration."

"You're embarrassing me. I couldn't find work around here even if I tried, which is not too damn likely. Bouchee, get down." My crazed Springer found Jamie to be a kindred soul and was leaping on her with practiced abandon. Two of a kind.

"He's alright, aren't you Bouchee?"

"Jamie, why did you really bring up the Finchley Boys last week? I've been thinking about that off and on ever since it happened. It's been nagging at me."

"I thought it might. *Hurt In Love*, John dear. The answer to the third reason for the tattoo. The singer was not what he seemed, you know. Maybe he'd been to Denmark. Get my drift?"

Oh shit. I think I did. I was beginning to believe that life was so far off the wall that the bizarre was actually normal. The hell with it. Play 'em as they lie.

"John, let's go fishing. You look like you need a break of sorts."

I did.

S · I · X

Adrift in the Dakotas

WE WERE LOST IN A LIQUID DESERT, not the endless miles of wind-blown sand and the devastating absence of either trees or water associated with the Gobi or Sahara. Here were multiple shades of blues and greens illuminated by the searing white of the sun pounding down relentlessly from a burned out sky. Even floating on cool water was a hot experience in this timeless wilderness. No breeze was blowing, and even if one was, we wouldn't know. The tall reeds and cattails stifled any air movement and trapped searing heat that was intensified as it reflected up from the glassy surface of the river. These pockets, small bays off the main stem of the Missouri, were miniature worlds isolated from the rest of the countryside. But at midday, they seemed lifeless. Ducks, geese, red-wing blackbirds—all gone, hunkered down somewhere in the shade. If our canoe had been made of aluminum, we would have been cooked by now, done to a turn: a South Dakota barbecue prepared for no one. As it was, we just sizzled quietly in the Royalex craft.

The idea of fishing seemed ludicrous; nothing would be moving in this blast furnace. Things were too bright out, anyway, but my guide insisted that I keep working my woolly bugger into small holes amid the clumps of vegetation. He said these openings marked upwellings of cool spring water, which

99

were magnets for forage fish and the smallmouth bass and northern pike that fed on them. I found this hard to believe and tossed the fly into one with all the enthusiasm of a George Dukakis supporter the day before the general election. The pattern hit the reeds and slid slowly down into the water. I let the thing sink for awhile, then began stripping it back without much interest. A sharp tug and the semblance of a set on my part, and I was fast to a smallmouth that ran around in determined circles before giving up and coming to net. A couple more and we were set. Slight intimations of angling enthusiasm appeared, so I worked the next spring more intently. Cast. Slide. Sink. Strip. Strike—another bass and then something else coming from out of nowhere with jet-like speed.

Ten feet from the canoe my fish was tagged by a northern: ripped to pieces, as ragged chunks of white flesh floated in the water made cloudy by the bass's blood. The pike swept past two more times, tearing another bit of meat, my fly, and the head of the fish along with a portion of the tippet. Any thoughts of jumping overboard for a quick dip were hastily abandoned, as I knew that northerns and muskies had slashed swimmers in Wisconsin and Minnesota. I saw no reason why the boys in this segment of the Missouri would behave any differently.

These were the first hours of a 40-mile float that would occupy four days. We'd drift through hundreds of thousands of acres of reed and cattail beds, wandering beneath sandstone bluffs and through wide-open prairie. We'd put in below the Fort Randall Dam and would take out at Santee, well above the Gavin's Point Dam. This part of South Dakota is wild, unspoiled land. Not often visited by the casual recreationist. Actually, most of the state is this way. Once off the interstate or other main highways, the countryside is sparsely populated with humans. Lakes and streams hold bass, pike, perch, northerns, tiger muskies, and trout. But the Dakotas get a bad rap from the ephemeral visitor, and that's fine, since this leaves more of the good life for the rest of us.

Dee Fondy, my guide and friend, first turned me on to this stretch of the Missouri a couple of years back when I was here as part of a state promotional affair, back when I had a brief relationship with the Outdoor Writers Association of America—a marriage dissolved by a lack of interest and an unwillingness to pay the high dues on my part. True, through my affiliation with OWAA, I did receive free samples of outdoor products, but how many cases of doe-in-heat deer urine does one man really need? Great gag gifts that wore a bit thin by the third Christmas. I'm being a bit hard on the organization; however, it's still hard to beat the exotic nature of the group's annual convention. But I digress as usual. Dee called one winter evening and asked if I wanted to float this part of the river some June. I said yes, and that's how we wound up here catching fish and making like a portable pig roast in Fondy's canoe.

The next three holes on the river turned smallmouth and, fortunately, no northerns. With the few smallmouth we had kept, dinner was covered, so we decided to move out into the current and drift down to a sand and gravel bar that offered some trees and shelter from the sun: a good place to spend the night according to Dee.

"We'll set up camp and take a siesta. We'll have covered about eight miles and that's plenty for today," said Dee as he maneuvered us through a narrow opening in the reeds. A great blue heron lifted off with quiet dignity as we passed a stranded tree near a raft of plant growth. The bird's wings beat slowly but with great power, and the heron was soon out of sight.

The Missouri flowed with surprising speed, propelling us downstream at six or more miles-per-hour. A slight suggestion of a breeze worked into our faces with cooling effect. The aquamarine water was still cool, influenced in part from the mountain snowmelt hundreds of miles to the west. Back home, the rivers of Montana would be running brown, turbid, and way out of control, what with trees and rocks crashing into eroding banks and bridge pilings and trout fighting for their lives or holed up in small feeder creeks. No fishing there for a few more weeks, at least. Here, however, everything was serene, peaceful. Wandering through a few hundred miles of the high plains can do that to a river, even one as large as the Missouri. The river is big in Montana, especially below Fort Peck Dam over east. But down here it is like a lake with current, and this is a relatively narrow piece of the water.

I've always been fascinated by the Missouri and its history, mostly the stuff about Lewis and Clark and their crew trying with admirable determination (some might even say obstinacy) to find a passage to the Pacific. To my way of thinking, a slightly crazed expedition vainly searching for a watery way across the continent. We all have our windmills to tilt at, but as noble as it may be, the notion of trying to drag a flat-bottomed barge up the Beaverhead and eventually over the Bitterroot Mountains is a bit out there in left field.

Also, the idea that some of the water we were floating on and in was originally snow and ice lying on the tops of peaks along Montana's Rocky Mountain front is intriguing. That's one of the fascinations of rivers for me: water moving from one part of the land, flowing through another region completely different from the headwaters and eventually winding up in the Gulf of Mexico or Hudson Bay or an ocean. I guess I'm easily amused. I've always wanted to float the entire Missouri but have had to settle for small stretches of the drainage: the Beaverhead by Dillon, Toston Dam to Toston. Craig to Cascade, Fort Benton to Loma, and the river below Fort Peck. And now this piece of water on the South Dakota-Nebraska border. I suppose it will all add up someday, but there are a lot of miles yet to see.

The fishing changes, too. Cutthroats live at the beginning in the small mountain freestone tributaries, then give way to strong rainbows and brutish browns. Further on are the warmwater species above Fort Peck, such as walleyes, catfish, bass, perch, and the regal carp, which just happens to be fair game on nymphs at times and excellent eating when properly smoked. And, of course, there are the pike and the small-mouths and some walleyes in the impoundments. Two thousand miles of changing conditions, an elaborate riverine personality—one of the main reasons so many of us are more easily drawn into the rhythms of moving water as opposed to still water and its concealed depths. Whatever; philosophical meditations on the "whys" of rivers and the religious aspects of flyfishing are largely ridiculous and most certainly noisome for many of us, though I sometimes find myself travelling these syrupy corridors. Hypocrisy is everywhere, even in me.

The bar was an island-sized affair and offered a hummock that rose gradually about 20 feet above the river. Cottonwoods grew here, as did an acre or so of lush grass. There were dandelions and even some clover. All in all, an excellent place to camp. Bugs probably wouldn't be a problem but we pitched the tent just in case, then rolled out tarps, pads, and sleeping bags in a clearing not far from a well-used fire ring, where there was plenty of dry, gray wood for tonight's conflagration. Nap time and then a little fishing before dinner.

I came to around five, not sure where I was, as usual. Dee was down below me cleaning the fish, so I wandered down.

"They're full of minnows and some crayfish," he said, as another chunky fillet landed in a tin pot. "Why don't you try a big streamer down below where the current meets up on the point. Always a few northerns there working the baitfish."

Fondy was right as I caught a few in the five- to seven-pound range. He was a meticulous guide and knew his river well. He'd started out as a walleye specialist on the lake above the dam by Yankton but quickly grew bored with "dragging license plates behind a boat" all day long. He found himself gravitating to the bass and pike and slowly learning the secrets of the river. He'd earned a solid reputation with a growing number of serious flyfishers, individuals who chased down out-of-the-way, unusual, isolated action. He knew how to make you laugh when the fish were somewhere else and the bugs weren't or when a cold rain was making minutes seem like miserable weeks. And he'd become an accomplished fly-fisherman and fly tier in only a few years. When I first fished with him, he was making the transition from baitcasting gear to ultra-light equipment. He'd never flyfished before, but after I managed to take a few smallmouths with a 4-weight, he wanted a try. He was casting more than adequately within minutes despite my help (a natural), and the first bass came in a hurry. Dee was thrilled and fascinated at once. The action of a gamefish resisting a fly rod is different, foreign to someone used to the feel of other rods. And working a streamer puts an angler more directly in the hunt, or so it seems to me. I could tell that a religious conversion was taking place with the fervor and rapidity that only another true believer could appreciate. We caught a lot of bass that day and the next and the next and a few northerns on streamers. Dee's showing me this virtually unknown smallmouth habitat led me to blow off the OWAA convention that I'd originally planned to attend somewhere in Iowa. And after leaving Dee, I fished my way back home in the Black Hills, Yellowstone, and the rivers Jamie and I had worked on her move from Jackson. All this was far more productive and enjoyable than standing around talking with some marginal lunatic dressed in a camouflaged suede sport coat discussing topics ranging from waterproofing boots to how to get $50 for a 3,000-word article on the art of making stink bait. All well and good to be sure, but four days of this kind of thing is a little much, and as I said, I decided on the Yankton trip. OWAA could go its way and I'd stumble along on mine, although the president-elect did inform me over the phone not long after my return home that my career would suffer irreparable harm if I dropped out of the organization. He was probably right: my truck is 12 years old; my income would make a 30-year-old arbitrageur snicker; and I can't seem to place an article in *Fur, Fins and Feathers...*Someday. But at least I'm respected in my own home town. Fantasies can be fun in a delusional way.

I got back to camp around seven, when the heat of the day was waning and a pleasant breeze was working upstream. Bank swallows were out swooping along the river eating mayflies and other bugs. Dozens of them loop-to-looped, barrel rolled, plummeted toward the water, and skimmed the surface standing on their wings. It looked like a miniature World War I dogfight. In the pink ochre dirt and sandstone bank on the north side of the river, hundreds of holes pockmarked the earth. Yellow warblers flitted around the reeds, and far above. A Northern harrier hung on the air and circled slowly, the dark and light banding of its tail visible, barely. Dee had a nice fire going with a pile of charcoal briquettes glowing gray red off to one side.

"Thought fried bass, sliced potatoes with onions baked in foil, and a salad of dandelion greens and wild onions would work. Sound okay?"

Seemed fine to me. This time of year the days ran long, and we had hours to go before dark. Time to enjoy a leisurely meal and turn into a vegetable while lounging around the fire. Perhaps a cigar would be in order. From this rise in the middle of the Missouri, I felt like we were all alone in the world, tripped back 100 years or more. No sounds of traffic. No power lines. No farms. We were alone. The salad was tasty in a slightly bitter way with a dressing of olive oil and lime juice. The bass was sweet. I wished we'd caught a few more. The sky was softening now, turning shades of orange, vermilion, and pink above the hills upriver. Time passed quickly but without hurry, an apparent contradiction common to float trips, and later, stretched out on my sleeping bag on the spongy grass, I watched the wood burn into constantly shifting worlds constructed of radiant coals and smoking limbs. It was easy to disappear into a fire. I must have dozed off.

We floated at our leisure the next day, wandering through the reeds, drifting at a pace that turned timeless, as only the river, the sky, birds, and the fish were noticed. We caught countless smallmouths in places I'm sure no one had ever fished before. And there were the pike, slashing and ripping their way through our leaders and streamers, tearing at the poor smallmouths that died as foul a death as the first. It was a gruesome sight that was hard to watch and impossible to turn away from. Each time a pike killed a smallmouth in a merciless charge, shivers rippled across my back and up my neck: a primal experience. Where were the pansy-assed animal rights freaks (the right word) when I wanted them? We again kept enough (more than the day before) bass for dinner and pitched camp on an island like the first one. They were all the same. The river never changed, either, flowing with ease and power toward the Mississippi. We could have been anywhere, nowhere. Just gliding along with no sense of self and a sharp sense of place.

After eating, straightening up (camp, that is), and building drinks, we resumed a conversation that we'd begun earlier in the day, one that we carried along with us in bursts and unanswered monologues. The best of guides seem to have developed an elaborate questioning philosophy regarding the natural world. Dee was no exception. As the talk intensified I asked him if I might tape what was rapidly turning into a one-sided discourse. He agreed and I scrounged my little machine from the camera bag. Imagine the following taking place under a gracefully deepening evening sky, the river making water sounds in the background, the fire popping, tin cups clinking against bottlenecks, and salient points punctuated with exclamations of approval from bodily orifices. At the time of this trip, Montana had recently closed fishing for native bull trout (my favorite salmonid species) because of drastically reduced numbers. The whole situation had caught the guide's attention since the matter was well covered in the media. This was the issue that had spawned our intermittent dialogue earlier. What follows is mostly Dee speaking and is accurately transcribed with only a few changes for continuity and minor deletions for the sake of waning coherency that increased in direct proportion with the degree of darkness. No paradox here.

"You know John, that recent closure of the fishing season for bull trout in your part of the state graphically demonstrates the political clout some of nature's species wield in the manipulative, often venal world of human beings. Your DNR (Montana Department of Fish, Wildlife, and Parks) responded to data that seemed to indicate that numbers of the fish had fallen to dangerously low levels in rivers such as the Flathead and Blackfoot. So the boys put a swift end to all angling for these brook trout brothers. Even out here in the middle of nowhere, I read about it in the papers and outdoor magazines, even on the local fishing talk shows, and God, are those things awful. But don't get me started.

"The fact that the closure will have little effect on the fate of the wild bulls as long as other deleterious environmental factors continue is a matter of some concern to an inveterate flyfisher such as myself, but not nearly as troubling and perplexing as a larger dilemma posited by a question like, 'Would mountain whitefish have created all this furor?' or 'What if the species threatened with extinction was the northern squaw-fish?' Would any of us give a damn? Would anybody really care? I wonder.

"And that is the heart of the matter, the real rub. Are we humans subconsciously anthropomorphizing the feral, natural world through our championing of glamorous species such as trout or grizzlies or by the enormous amounts of emotional, physical, and financial energy we expend to protect cute, fuzzy, cuddly animals such as pandas, black-footed ferrets, and spotted owls? Notwithstanding the havoc our exploding numbers are wreaking on the planet, are we creating an unnatural vision of the world by coming to the rescue of leopards, tigers, elephants, Atlantic salmon, pileated woodpeckers, and blue whales at the expense of lesser lights such as brown recluse spiders, assorted worms and eels, and little-known rodents?

"Are we turning the earth, especially designated wilderness areas, into designer zoos, places choking in a miasma of mediocre sameness? What does this say about us as a species? Are we so far gone, so chauvinistic, that even our well-intentioned acts are fraught with hidden desires to dominate, shaded with a genetically-driven need to ruin a world and remake it to our own specifications or, more frightening, a twilight zone replication of our own image?

"If this is indeed true, the ramifications are daunting. Our decisions concerning which species will be granted survival and which ones will be allowed to perish, possibly from not so benign neglect, are suspect. Further, are we so afraid of really living in the natural world, so fearful of perishing at the fangs of some diminutive reptile or poorly publicized arachnid, that we are making decisions that will transform our world into something more homogenous, something less terrifying—a juiceless Disneyland nightmare experience?

"Not only can the truth hurt, but in the case of the natural environment, it can be horrifying. Very few of us seem to want any serious contact with the "real" world, one filled with life forms that instill us with a sense of loathing and even repulsion. The fact that this environment is rife with bloody, carnivorous violence and random, death-dealing events such as earthquakes, typhoons, and avalanches is largely ignored by most of us, especially those inculcated with the dogma of political correctness.

"I am not an apologist for my own kind, the type of tragic person who derides the human race, all the while trying to separate himself from this malevolent horde by loudly listing the numerous atrocities our species has committed in a brief span of time—in mere millennia. This position reeks of emotional insecurity and societal posturing, certainly not reasoned concern or visceral passion. Far from it. Admittedly, I burn fossil fuels, eat red meat with relish, do not spend time plotting the overthrow of imperialistic *America* (which, from what I gather listening to many, is the entity responsible for most of the earth's woes), and would be less than upset if all leeches, black flies, and red-rumped baboons vanished from the world. Still, I see tremendous capacity in humans to solve labyrinthine problems, to even at times display a certain spiritual elegance.

"In short, am I the type of person I have just been wondering about, the kind that is willing to devote large amounts of time trying to save an idyllic trout stream or an old-growth forest while turning my back on a developer's ruthless plan to drain some malarial bog filled with myriad but unappreciated life forms? If this is so, what am I really thinking? What are my real motives? Are they pure or are they tainted with the stain of self-aggrandizement? Are we all to varying degrees this type of person? Evidence suggests that the answer is 'YES.'

"Consider the organizations formed and supported by sportsmen. There are Pheasants Forever, The Ruffed Grouse Society, Ducks Unlimited, and Trout Unlimited, to name a few. Is there a Mottled Dog, Whelk Forever or a Mountain Sucker Unlimited? I've yet to hear of a Black Widow Society, though I may be out of the loop on this one. And then there are groups such The Wilderness Society, Sierra Club, and Greenpeace that seem to be far more concerned with the glamour species while offering mere lip service for the lesser-known creatures of our world.

"If the animal and/or its surroundings are not exotic, majestic, or beautiful, do we really care about them?

"Some may point to the snail darter and the proposed Tellico Dam on the Little Tennessee River. Look at all the out-cry the possible elimination of that one insignificant creature caused, critics of my position might say. The fish was even on the nightly network news as Tom hurked and jerked his way through reading the teleprompter. True, but the dam was built anyway, and that one strain of darter was left drifting moribund in the new structure's swirling tailwaters. Who really cared about this downscale member of the *Percidae* family? After all, there are nearly 150 other species of darter. Well, you can be damn sure that if the Little Tennessee River contained a population of 20-pound bass or trophy rainbow trout that would be wiped out by the dam, that thing would not have been built.

"To survive in this climate you need glitz, hype, the potential to make some industry (say sporting, environmental or tourism) big bucks, and you need the support of a well-monied constituency. Without these attributes, the darters, Texas toads, and Northern bog lemmings don't stand a chance.

"Environmentalism is a big-time business right now. The days of fighting an issue on its merits alone are pretty much shot. Large conservation organizations are far more likely to lend both legal and financial support to protecting grizzly habitat or stopping a whale hunt, but a brutal roundup and exploitation of rattlesnakes in the southwest goes largely unchallenged (and unnoticed until Audubon staffer Ted Williams did a subtle evisceration of the event). And I've never heard of anyone wearing snakeskin boots having blood or red paint tossed on them as has happened to so many fur wearers. Defenders of Wildlife, Fund For Animals, and similar entities focus their attentions on situations involving high visibility species such as bison and the nearly ubiquitous grizzly dilemma, and of course those splashing, dashing whales. These beings are the darlings of the media. They are the natural world stars. Bright lights and hyperbolic print mean cash. Organizations by their very nature run the money trail, noses tight to the scent. The more wealth they accumulate, the more clout they have when it comes to protecting our favorite animals and pieces of unspoiled turf (and the greater the salaries those in control can pay themselves). Most of this is all well and good. A world without *Ursus horribilis* and *Balaenoptera musculus* would be a diminished place, but what about the web-toed salamanders of the planet?

"The argument, which states that by protecting creatures at the top of the food chain, we also wind up saving the rest of the systems has some merit, but is not air tight. It is quite possible to re-introduce wolves to the upper Midwest while the Wood turtle's fragile habitat, and swiftly following, the animal itself, disappears from sight. And what about human beings, the species that sits atop this pyramid with regal imperiousness? We thrive at the expense of the world's existence. Some species ARE more adaptable and smarter than others. I think that one of the chief reasons we fight the so-called good fight for lions, tigers, bears, old-growth forest, coastal shorelines, and grassy prairies is because these things are easily assimilated into our way of life, our world view. Visions of oceans of emerald grasses turning softly sere on a late summer breeze or ridge after ridge carpeted with pine forest filled with bears and wolves and crystalline streams holding colorful trout are more to our way of thinking. They are less threatening to our fragile hold on sanity than a reality that also embraces tractless swamps, harsh deserts, and alkali flats that stretch off into an eternal distance.

"Consider what Cormac McCarthy said in his brutally honest novel, *Blood Meridian*, a book about the Tex-Mex border of the 1850s.

> ...They watched storms out there so distant they could not be heard, the silent lightning flaring sheetwise and the thin black spine of the mountain chain fluttering and sucked away in the dark. They saw wild horses racing on the plain, pounding their shadows down the night and leaving in the moonlight a vaporous dust like the palest stain on their passing.

"Admittedly, this country does not provide the sylvan beauty of Yellowstone National Park in July, the beauty slightly-crazed visitors observe through the safety of car windshields and camera viewfinders a tamed landscape filled with animals inured to human attention. Nor does this landscape offer the surreal delights of Yosemite and its clouds of noxious automobile exhalations during the height of summer gridlock.

"What McCarthy's vision does offer is an undisciplined excursion into what is wild, unfathomable, and magic. The alkali flats, the desert, the few unspoiled mountain ranges present images that trip back far beyond even the embryonic stirrings of our hunter-gatherer heritage. They are at once soulfully terrifying and exciting, intoxicating stuff that we turn our backs on, like slamming the door of our homes on a dark, storming night. Give us coffee table books filled with photographs of raccoons, monarch butterflies, elephants, bald eagles—even cape buffalo—but whatever you do, do not expose us to the entirety of the real world. God no. Let us pick and choose that which most resembles ourselves, those objects which our minds can readily digest and assimilate into human form and behavior patterns, that which pleases and comforts us.

"Silent storms on empty alkali flats, giant worms slithering through the primordial ooze of a Borneo jungle—Are you out of your mind? I'll look at the pictures, quickly, but I'm busy saving the elk and the whales and the salmon. They truly need our help. And so the unappreciated species go, ghosting silently from our awareness as we move one step farther from the natural world, our true home.

"Spending less than a minute going through my collection of books one day last winter, I turned up titles on black and grizzly bears, and wolves—one on endangered animals featuring a panda on the cover. Another on natural history picturing a bald eagle and old-growth forest. Still another with an elk grazing near a river at sunset and yet one more, this time with a deer standing majestically in the honeyed light of late afternoon. Where were the books with photos of suckers, rodents, and bugs? To be honest, I wouldn't buy many of those. Nor would most of us. We like to focus on and adopt animals, places, and causes that are close to our hearts. Publishers, conservation groups, and the media know this and they are out to make a buck as quickly and painlessly as possible. Who is going to proudly display a glossy tome depicting a Conger eel on its cover, a creature not likely to engender appropriate conversation over martinis, white wine, and those cute miniature spinach quiches during a weekend party.

" 'Good god! What is that ugly thing?' " a guest might ask in obvious revulsion.

" 'Oh, that's a great new book on creatures of the coastal swamps,' the host replies.

" 'That makes me sick,' the queasy visitor responds, and the book vanishes from sight as does any notice of the poor, slimy eel. Conversation turns more to sedate, time-tested topics like a recent llama pack trip in South America or the state of the Republican Party.

"The same holds true for the land itself. I have beautiful books on Patagonia, Lake Baikal, Montana, Yosemite, Yellowstone, the Grand Canyon, and four thousand titles on mountains. I've just two on deserts and one on swamps. I've surrounded myself with books that reflect a vision of the world that is at once reassuring but also one that isolates me from the environment. I'm out of touch with the natural order of things. I love trout streams, this river we're floating now.

Don't bother me with arid wastes. Perhaps we can irrigate that land and make it useful, fill it with deer and elk and raptors.

"That's how most of us see the natural world, a place filled with bucolic, controlled splendor and not a place of harsh reality, brutal climate, and heartless predators. That is a truth too difficult to contemplate or even marginally grasp for most of us. As a result, those undisciplined places and the species that inhabit them suffer, vanishing not from overpopulation and pollution, but rather from isolation, by being cut off from the entire phony, protective process, or by our constant meddling and tinkering with them. Radio-controlled bears. Give me a break. How would you feel wandering around with a 10-pound collar of transistors, plastics, and duct tape wrapped around your neck? Try picking up a woman in a bar or getting your Visa card approved at a bank.

"There are those who will say that many of us love the desert and places like it. To them I say what about the White Sands Missile Range in New Mexico and the Idaho National Engineering Lab (a U.S. Atomic Energy Commission Reservation) located just north of scenic downtown Atomic City-population 34 and dropping. Driving through that country gives me the radiation creeps. We've perverted it, given the countryside an alien spin that may be a truer reflection of our inner beings than all the National Parks in North America and beyond. These places are unhealthy, charged with high-tech malevolence. We make jokes about these blasted, radiated locations. We erect twisted monuments, propose bizarre national parks intended to venerate our madness. Imagine the response turning the Smoky Mountains or Grand Canyon National Park into one of these nuclear sites would provoke. We're talking 1968 Democratic Convention days of rage intensity here. Screwing with wasted, arid chunks of desert is one thing. Messing around with our mountains, forests, and rivers is another. We cherish what is obviously beautiful and, even in its most primal state, this hallowed ground appears relatively unthreatening to our collective psyche. In doing this, we turn our backs on what is strange, grotesque, and too difficult to fully comprehend, moving still farther from the unavoidable truth waiting out in the wide open for us.

"Or take a look at Banff National Park in Canada. Take a good look. Talk about trashed, human style. Spectacular scenery quickly gives way to an overall impression of tamed subservience. Networks of roads running level and smooth service backcountry outfitters' camps. Regulations prohibit almost everything. Hordes of us ride worn-out horses or slog along manure-clogged trails in search of solitude. We've turned something pristine and wonderful into our own vision and in the process have created an ugly postcard.

"While some chosen species survive, if not actually thrive, under our self-perceived, benevolent ministrations, others will be obliterated, walking out of existence unnoticed by us as we concernedly do the right thing for the planet while drifting ever so steadily away from the ways of the natural world and into the comfort and conceptual convenience of our Manifest Destiny.

"The way things are going, the situation may soon become weird enough to satisfy even the discriminating tastes of Hunter Thompson or Newt Gingrich.

"Where in the hell is the damn mother ship? Abandoned once again."

Guides are a varied lot, but I've never met a good one yet who hasn't had his or her own well-formed perspective on the nature of things. Obviously, Fondy was no exception, as this soliloquy demonstrated.

By now the sky was glowing with billions of stars, galaxies, and other objects. We talked a little about fishing and sports and tomorrow's activities before turning in.

The next day was clear once again and promised to be even hotter than the first two. By eight the temperature was in the 80s and just loading the canoe was a warming experience. We spent endless hours moving downstream, fishing a little, and talking even less.

Toward the end of that day's cruise, we pulled over to shore below a long, deep run that flowed from the end of an eddy. Fondy said to rig up with sink tips and weighted hare's ear nymphs, both on the point and the dropper. I had no idea what we were after and he wouldn't tell me.

We then cast the patterns up into the foaming swirl and let the flies work to the bottom. The current was strong to the point that we were forced to add a couple of split-shot (steel, of course) and in a few minutes I noticed Fondy's rod tip bob up and down and he set the hook. Then his rod bent in the shape of a "U" and something large and powerful was obviously on the end of the line. Whatever the fish was, it soon turned downstream and made run after run out into the main course of the river. Eventually, the thing tired and Dee pulled it to shore. It was a carp, flashing brown and golden with a hint of red in its fins. Big lips pulsating open and closed in the shallow water of the sandy beach.

"A little variety never hurts," Fondy said. "I've caught them here almost 20 pounds before. Great sport and the fillets taste okay if you spice them up a bit with Tabasco, salt, and pepper. Not really killing the taste, just modifying it some."

We worked the spot for another hour, and I managed to beach one of maybe five pounds. Fondy took three more up to 10 pounds. All these fish were strong fighters in a work-man-like way: a lot of fun. I've always had a soft spot in my heart (or head?) for carp, having chased them with whiskey-flavored doughballs on the Rock River in northern Illinois many years ago as a kid. I'd actually placed first two years in a row with my friend Big Hudge in the Unlimited Class of the annual Rock River International Carp Derby. One of our carp even finished second in the time trials held at the check-in station. The fish were dropped into a long, galvanized metal tank filled with running water and a stopwatch was used to see how long it took the carp to move from one end to the other. Our thoroughbred covered the distance of 40 feet in just under a minute. A magnificent effort that brought a roar from the crowd of 13 or 14 hapless onlookers. Those were the days.

And that's the way the last day went, too: drifting and fishing and taking in whatever the Missouri had to show us. We'd only been out for four days, but the trip seemed like it lasted only an hour. I helped Dee with the canoe and other gear, loaded up my belongings, then accompanied the guide to a waterside cafe for a cheeseburger and a beer before turning around to drive back home at a leisurely pace. As we parted, Dee promised to come visit later in the year, maybe in early September.

I never saw him again.

About a year after the trip, on a whim, I called his number in Yankton to say "hello." The line had been disconnected. Several calls to friends who knew Fondy revealed a sad story. His wife, apparently tired of the long hours he kept and the paycheck-to-paycheck existence, had pulled up stakes, leaving with their three children, filing for divorce, and moving in with her mother on the East Coast. Fondy grew despondent, let his business lapse, and began to drink heavily. One night while driving home after closing time, he missed a corner at high speed and slammed into a telephone pole out in the cornfields west of town. The truck burst into flames and extinguished Fondy.

Dee was a great guy and I wouldn't wish those lonely months or the way he died on anybody. I'd miss floating the Missouri with him and the chance to show him some of my favorite rivers and lakes in Montana. I'd miss his long, rambling discourses on everything from the natural world to politics to why left-handers could not play third base.

Most of all, I'd miss the man himself. One way or the other, guys like him are facing extinction. Hell, we all are.

S·E·V·E·N

They're All Crazy in Dillon

THE BEAVERHEAD IS AN HONEST RIVER. If you fish it properly, most of the time you will catch trout. If you don't, most of the time you won't catch trout.

Unlike many streams, the Beaverhead is rarely forgiving in nature. There are times of insect activity (summer's cranefly extravaganza comes to mind) when the browns and rainbows lose some of their innate caution and make a spectacle of themselves, crashing about the surface as they charge up from dark water running beneath dense tangles of bankside brush, hammering flies with impressive enthusiasm. Most of the time my limited success on the river has come from working nymphs with extreme concentration or pounding large streamers tight to shore, frequently loosing my skillfully-tied woolly buggers in the bushes, or, when a brown takes, losing the fish in those same bushes' submerged and exposed root balls. But I keep trying.

Perhaps it is the hardcore personality of the river, or perhaps it is something in the water, but the guides I've fished with on the Beaverhead are a breed unto themselves. Great guys who are also friends of mine, but that doesn't stop them from constantly pointing out the few weaknesses in my prodigious angling skills with a biting sense of humor. Many guides will just give in to a client's weaknesses after the first hours of

119

obvious futility, as they realize that some of us are beyond redemption. I mean, they *know* there are fish where I've just dropped my fly with a delicacy that resembles a watermelon heaved from a height of 10 feet. But not so with the boys from Dillon. They see these inept actions of mine as a challenge, and they never let up. By the end of the day I am a whipped soul, head hanging low and the distant call of a cold drink and a warm meal my only possible hope for salvation. The thing is, I always have a good—no, a *great*—time with these guys, and when I return to my home waters up north I find that I am fishing more attentively and thoroughly (though this brief upward blip in my angling acumen rapidly washes away as old bad habits regain their hold on me once again).

The first time I floated the Beaverhead with one of these southwest Montana flyfishing mavens was years ago on a dark and dreary day in mid-October. It was so long ago, in fact, that I still had a good deal of hair growing on top of my head. I mean, this was way back when the Cubs had won their first divisional title (only to be robbed of the pennant by some late-inning antics by the Padres' Steve Garvey). The weather was slate-gray cold with little wind. My companion was, and still is, a writer for a major magazine, but he shall remain nameless in the interests of his job security. Our guide, Charlie Grimm, was a happy, bearded soul of athletic construction. He had Jimmy Buffett blasting from his truck's stereo as we motored to the river. My friend, we'll call him José, and I had been up late the night before playing pool and sampling the wonders of Dillon's nightlife. Suffice it to say that things were foggy by the time we made it back to our motel room, but I do remember that a couple of hefty women found both José and me quite amusing. I honestly have no idea why, as my pool game was certainly nothing remarkable, and it couldn't have been our snappy repartee. We had fun all the same. So when the crack of 10 a.m. rolled around, we were ready in a laid-back sort of way.

Gear was assembled, loaded, and the raft launched. José manned the front, Grimm handled the oars, and I held forth in the back. We cast to all the right-looking places for a quarter-mile or so without luck before pulling over to work a prime, deep riffle and a nice pool. Charlie casted over to the head of the run with a pair of weighted nymphs, and on about the 40th cast, a huge rainbow tagged the point fly and pancaked its way downstream, thrashing and smacking the surface of the surprised river. Grimm managed to corral the trout about 50 yards downstream beneath a cloying clump of brush. José worked below the struggling fish and scooped it up in a huge net—six pounds or more of dark silver, mean red, and severe green with intense black spotting—a serious rainbow.

I never would have pounded that run for that length of time with that degree of thoroughness, but that's what it takes on the Beaverhead sometimes. We fished hard until around two, then broke for lunch. The fishing was off. I'd turned a brown that flashed briefly behind my bugger before high-tailing it beneath the bank. José had several short strikes. That was it. Time for cold, fried chicken, coleslaw, and some delicious Schmidt beer; they don't brew any better. The three of us got along well, giving each other healthy doses of grief punctuated with the appropriate hand and finger motions. Intellectual communication at its finest.

The day went along at this slow angling pace until a large brown, over 24 inches, tagged my black bugger. The fish fought out in the middle of the river, and Grimm quickly beached the raft on an open piece of gravel shoreline. The trout fought doggedly and with strength before the guide waded out and netted it. I was shaking right along with José, but managed to take a number of shots that turned out surprisingly well. In fact, one shot graces the cover of my first book, *Knee Deep in Montana's Trout Streams*: a great photo and layout that makes the brown look like an outlaw on a wanted poster hanging in the local post office: an archetypal Beaverhead brown trout. The fish made my day and I retired to the front of the raft to sip Schmidt, smoke cigars, and give José a hard time. He was having one of those memorable outings where he did everything right except setting the hook. While this has never happened to me, I understand the frustration and can sympathize (not empathize) with said angler's irritation when something like this all-too-common shortcoming occurs.

The day turned toward evening and the cold grew colder. We pulled off the water and headed into town for some needed refreshment and excellent steaks at the Bannack House. Another late night ensued, at first with Grimm in tow, then José and I under Charlie's care. A fine time was had by all.

Since that initial foray, I have had the opportunity to fish with Grimm and his friend Pete Reiser, owner of an area fly shop, on several occasions. I've always caught at least a few decent trout, had a good time, learned some in the process, and had many spirited conversations while bobbing down the river. One gripe we all have in common is the animal rights wacko fanatics and their ever-escalating attack on hunting and, lately, flyfishing. Obviously, guides are somewhat against the position, in part because their livelihood is at stake, but more so, I think, it's because a way of life and an activity they dearly love is being threatened by those ignorant subnormals whose idea of a wild time is watching *Nature* on PBS. The extent of this end-all-fishing/hunting lunacy was pointed out to me on a recent Beaverhead float trip when Grimm detailed a recent article that appeared in that literary bastion of the natural world, *The Wall Street Journal.* I'm not sure if the *WSJ* endorsed the anti-sentiment that follows, but by publishing the odious viewpoint, the paper did lend an air of credence to this drivel.

As Grimm tells it, the article recounts how a poor soul named Jasper Thomas was fishing the Madison River in the Ennis area one morning, hoping, I assume, to catch a fat rainbow or brown, when the sky began to rain rocks-baseball-sized ones. The bewildered Jasper looked up to see two young men (I'm sure they were fine representatives of the human race) winging the projectiles in his direction.

"Hey, you'll scare the fish!" Jasper exclaimed. To which they replied, "That's the point."

The intrepid Jasper did the right thing. He ripped razor-like casts with deadly accuracy in the direction of the two nature lovers who fled in terror, but not before they had plastered his truck with antifishing leaflets. Obviously, the first amendment in all its glory under the Big Sky.

The story went on from there, explaining that the animal-rights movement has a new angle: It wants to ban fishing. Not just big commercial driftnet operations that pull in ton upon ton of fish, and unfortunately, dolphins and seals in the process. But the animal-rights ding-a-lings want to abolish all fishing, including Jasper's flyfishing on the Madison and presumably bass fishing in his home state of Texas as well. And they aren't stopping with just fish. The goal, say animal-rights leaders (a level-headed bunch who have taken the syllogistic process to new heights), is to spare the creatures from agonizing deaths (of which starving to death due to overpopulation apparently is not one).

"Just because fish and lobsters aren't cute and cuddly doesn't mean they don't suffer excruciating pain," said Tracy Reiman, an organizer with People for the Ethical Treatment of Animals, or PETA, a group of officious know-it-alls based in Washington, D.C. (where else?), that is spearheading the fish-rights campaign. "You wouldn't sink a hook into your cat and leave it flopping on the deck gasping for air, would you?" she asks. "You wouldn't boil it alive?'"

(A crazy friend of mine from Wichita, Kansas, sent me a copy of this *WSJ* story dated October 10, 1995. Not everything I write is fiction—for a copy send a money order in the amount of $39.95, made out to me, along with a SASE. The article arrived with a nice degree of synchronicity when I returned from the trip to the Beaverhead that included this discussion.)

I admit that it is difficult to argue with this compelling logic, but as the article and Grimm's grumblings pointed out, the whole situation doesn't get any saner.

Activists dressed in lobster suits have berated diners entering Gladstone's, a restaurant in Pacific Palisades, California, which serves as many as 10,000 lobsters a month. The nefarious Crustacean Liberation Front has tagged San Francisco cafes with pro-lobster graffiti. In England, underwater free-dom fighters in scuba gear have prowled the depths at fishing tournaments herding away trophy carp and snipping off lures.

The article continues, and I quote: "The campaign is bound to hit snags, given fishing's widespread popularity; an estimated 54 million people fish in America, including many members of Congress."

While I admit that I find the notion of pro-lobster graffiti somewhat intriguing and have always had a soft spot in my heart for carp, disrupting fishing tournaments strikes me as a bit ludicrous.

The reaction of anglers is more biting. "Those antifishing folks are cuckoo," said the venerable Virgil Ward, a member of three fishing Halls of Fame and former producer of weekly television fishing shows. Ward, in his 80s at the time, had recently retired so he could spend more time fishing. He says antifishing groups periodically send him letters asking him to join their cause. "They make me so damn mad I just throw 'em in the trash can," grumbled Ward. "Then I go fishing to calm down."

Grimm chuckled and opened another Schmidt. "The pro-fish forces were not deterred. PETA declared a National Fish Amnesty Day at Fisherman's Wharf in San Francisco. The fisherman were baited up and ready to go before dawn, and some guy named Antonio Caldera, a regular at the wharf, said 'Anybody tells me I can't fish, I consider making them bait.' I'm with Antonio 100 percent," said Grimm as he took a hit on his beer.

I am willing to admit that these anti- fools are persistent. One recent spring, PETA led a band of approximately 30 pro-testers to Anglin's Pier in Fort Lauderdale, Florida. Amid scattered boos and shouts of "Get a life!" the protesters waved banners reading "Fishing: Cold-blooded Sport" and "Get Hooked on Compassion, Not Fishing." Activists considered the outing a success, but then you have to cut a little slack for anyone who thinks wandering around dressed like a lobster is an effective form of protest. As the manager of Anglin's, Will

Harty, said "What these protesters don't understand is that people here love fishing more than anything—with the possible exception of their mamas."

All the same, we Americans are rank amateurs compared to fish-rights activists in England. In order to close down tournaments, the protesters flail the water with 20-foot bamboo poles to scatter the fish, not to mention the scuba brigade. A local borough council in South London tried banning fishing at Clapham Commons. Signs proclaiming "All Fishing Strictly Prohibited" were raised around the park's largest pond and were promptly ignored. "The anti-fishies are off their rockers," said Steven Jones, an out-of-work South Londoner, while he skillfully chummed the waters with maggots to attract fish. The ban was repealed.

While most of us, at one time or another, have spouted the old saw that fish feel no pain, scientific evidence refutes this and lends a small degree of credibility to the sentiments of organizations such as PETA. "They are sentient organisms, so of course they feel pain," said Dr. Austin Williams, a National Marine Fisheries Service zoologist. But Dr. Richard Rosenblatt, an ichthyologist at the Scripps Institution of Oceanography, notes that life at sea is naturally rough, and that getting caught and eaten by a fisherman is probably no worse than getting caught and eaten by a shark. "No sardine ever died a happy death," commented Rosenblatt.

"To say fishing is cruel is just ridiculous," said Ann Lewis, spokeswoman for the Bass Anglers Sportsman Society in Montgomery, Alabama, which is seeking a site for its theme park with a possible name of Bassanation Center. Virgil Ward adds, "Fishing cruel? That's the biggest fish story I've ever heard."

With all the hype, the potential for Hollywood types to jump on the feel-good, give-me-publicity bandwagon is growing. Consummate actress and devoted vegetarian Mary Tyler Moore hooked up with activists who defended Spike, a 70-year-old, 12-pound lobster, that was to be raffled off and eaten at Gladstone's restaurant. The redoubtable Ms. Moore offered

$1,000 to free Spike, prompting Rush Limbaugh to offer $2,000 to eat him. Gladstone's decided to keep Spike in his tank as a tourist attraction. The president of Gladstone's says his suppliers now have a new name for large lobsters: Mary Tyler Moores.

Ms. Moore's reaction: "Good. At least people are thinking about our message."

"People like Mary Tyler Moore are clueless," laughed Grimm. "They're idiots with Bambi mentalities. But they are having an impact on what people think. Get enough of those fools in the Eastern media to start buying her crap, and we may have a battle on our hands. I hope I'm alive and kicking when the bureaucrats try and outlaw hunting and fishing in Montana. That will be fun. Talk about a war."

You wonder if they've ever considered how much wildlife habitat has been destroyed to make the airports and runways their private jets land on or how much destruction has been visited on the planet in the extraction and burning of fossil fuels to power the engines that make their (our) mobile lives possible. I wonder how many trees are cut down to make my books (and theirs). Banning flyfishing and hunting is, at best, a simplistic approach that plays well at Beverly Hills cocktail parties. I'm with Grimm, and it would be fun to raise a little (or a lot) of hell with the East Coast effete (call me Spiro) and the overpaid Hollywood brain dead. One can dream.

Not all of my fishing around Dillon has taken place on the Beaverhead. Twenty-five miles west of town and south of the Pioneer Mountains flows Grasshopper Creek, a small stream that meanders through rolling, sere hills of sage, native grasses, and through fields of hay. Bannack, the first territorial capitol of Montana, is now a ghost town turned state park. This is where a good deal of the state's history took place, complete with robbers (the infamous Plummer Gang), hangings, whores, and carousing—all the good stuff.

The year before I'd driven a pickup truck down from a then-operating gold mine with the place's owner. Sitting in my lap was a five-gallon bucket filled with a mixture of water, mud, and as it turned out later, over $35,000 in gold dust and flakes. The most real money I've ever had my hands on. The mine soon went belly up, and the owner fled to Alaska in search of his elusive fortune.

A dirt road follows Grasshopper Creek much of the way. And in the canyon below Bannack and the undercut-bank stretches above, there is plenty of holding water for brown trout that reach a couple of pounds or more. Early in the summer there are prodigious flocks of blood-thirsty mosquitoes. This is also rattlesnake country, which always seem to be present in great numbers wherever fine trout waters exist.

One early July afternoon, Grimm and I hauled our act to the stream and began working small hopper imitations. This was rushing the season a bit, but fair numbers of the bugs were clacking, leaping, and soaring along the banks. Grimm rigged up and worked downstream, while I started casting my way against the slight current. In an hour, I took several browns to 16 inches on short casts next to the grassy banks. The trout pounced on the bushy pattern and then tried to streak back to shelter. I was in love with this stream—all of the fish were fat, golden, and eager.

A few yards ahead, a pile of rocks and a downed tree blocked my path, so I exited the water and started walking through the tall grass and yellowish bare patches of rocky earth. A pair of browns were hammering hoppers as the insects landed awkwardly on the water, sucking them in with slurpy gulps, as I bent over, hands on knees, to watch the activity. Somewhere in the back of my consciousness a soft hissing, shaking sound registered. Not right away but over a period of seconds. I looked down in front of me and there was a coiled rattlesnake, tinted in shades of malevolent ochres and the softest, nastiest looking green. The reptile's head was extended, its wired yellowish eyes boring into me. Its rattle was rattling and I freaked, lurching backwards, pirouetting on one foot and doing a spastic ballet as fast as my uncoordinated movements would allow me. The hair on my neck and arms was charged with the electricity of primal fear. I was back at the truck before

I knew it, shaking as I rummaged around in the dark recesses
of the cooler for a Schmidt. I popped the sucker open, and
never has a beer tasted so good or the foam felt so cool and fine
running down my chin. My hands were cut and bleeding. The
knee of my jeans was ripped. One Converse All Star looked like
a semi's blown retread lying dead on the Interstate. My helter-
skelter escape must have looked like a bad scene from an old
Andy Clyde movie, or worse. There is something about ven-
omous snakes that reduces me to pure terror and kicks me into
the flee-like-hell survival mode. The closest sensation is that of
a thousand feet of exposure on the side of a mountain; neither
experience is one I enjoy.

Grimm showed up in the middle of my next can of beer
and asked why I was so white and nervous. When I explained,
he laughed and said they scared the crap out of him, too. But
despite the snakes, I've fished Grasshopper a couple of times
since then, always with good results for the browns and always
with a sharp eye peeled for the rattlers.

We drove south, farther into the uninhabited hills, past
crumbling wood flumes that were used nearly a century ago to
bring water to the mine locations. The road was narrow, rutted. We kicked up a cloud of salmon-colored dust that hung
like a curtain in the still air. Eventually we pulled up to a small
stream with the wonderful name of Bloody Dick Creek. I never
was able to discover the origin of the appellation, but my imagination has come up with an idea or two.

Grimm knew the rancher where we were going to fish, so
we paid no heed to the bullet riddled No Trespassing signs that
were hammered into the weathered fence posts that supported
limp strands of rusty barbed wire. The creek was not wide but
had some nice holes. The water whirled and glided darkly. The
gentle movements of trout working in the current were barely
discernible as the fish undulated slowly back and forth just
above the streambed. A truly mysterious, silent motion. I tied
on an Adams and took brook trout after brook trout to perhaps a foot or a little more. Trout raced up to slash at the bobbing fly, making little splashes in the process. The fish were full

of color as only brookies can be—turquoise, emerald, orange, vermilion, copper, jet black, virgin white. They were easy marks. Any cast that even approached a suggestion of holding water turned a trout, and as it turned out, we each caught dozens that afternoon, Grimm said that he thought I might need to regain my confidence after yesterday's efforts on the river, and he thought that this little number would turn the trick. He was right, but I ignored him all the same and enjoyed the ride back into town. We pulled up in front of the Bannack House and disembarked for the obligatory martinis and rare steaks. A person could spend his life doing this. Grimm agreed and said that some of us even fake it at making a living flyfishing.

In the title of this chapter, I said they're all crazy in Dillon; yet, I mean this in the best of ways. Guides walk a wavering tightrope with their clients. Each day they have to almost instantly size up the clients with whom they will be spending a day on the river. Will the people be easy to get along with or are they going to be hardasses who expect to be treated like visiting royalty and also expect to catch large numbers of trophy trout? Can they cast? Read water? Do they have senses of humor, or are they wired to a surly pitch clinging to dreadful baggage of unfulfilled and less than happy lives? All tough questions that psychiatrists charge good money to answer with varying degrees of success. A guide's income depends on his ability to assess his clients. And then there are the fish and the bugs. What if the rainbows have virtually stopped feeding, or the day is so clear and hot that the few caddis that do hatch race off the water like rockets while the trout hide from the intense light?

The boys from Dillon handle this dilemma with apparent ease, instantly adjusting to the mood swings that always accompany the flickering fortunes of angling. They love to fish, but what they do is work, except on rare occasions when those in the raft with them have fished enough to know that you play the ball as it lies. Take the good with the bad and it all turns into fun. I've been lucky to fish much more than most, and I

have a sweet disposition—just ask my ex-wife. So Grimm and
Reiser can relax and be themselves when I have the rare opportunity to spend some time with them. Catching large fish, any
fish, is fun, but only a small part of the game. Some good-
natured kidding, a little casting, a lot of BS, and a few beers:
easy times among good people. This is the way things should
be. Not the attitude that has spawned atrocities like international flyfishing competitions ("Go USA") or social abortions
masquerading as flyfishing that cost a few thousand a pop to
enter with the express purpose of trying to see which yo-yo can
catch the most fish on one fly and impress the designated
celebrities (at least in their own minds). This type of idiocy
belongs on TV or in Miami (is there a difference here?), not on
a trout stream. My favorite guides feel the same way. I can see
it in their eyes as they drink in the landscape, or the way they
light up when someone in the raft connects with a hefty cutthroat, or when a pair of nesting sandhill cranes is spotted on a
small grassy island. They know what the good stuff is all about.

One curiosity I've noticed among guides, those from
Montana in particular, is that many of them (over half) jok-
ingly or more often seriously, believe in the existence of
extraterrestrial life. I can't remember all of the conversations
about UFO sightings, and the plausibility of alien visitations
I've had on the water. Maybe my own strange madness brings
this out in otherwise normal individuals. I admit to being a
firm believer in the concept that the human race is a failed
experiment; I myself am still waiting for the mother ship.
While none of us has ever claimed to participating in an alien
abduction (at least not publicly), some of us fervently believe
in life on other planets. Perhaps spending so much time completely free in wild, unspoiled, beautiful country leads to this.
Or maybe the type of person who sacrifices security to make
a living outside is prone to these wonderings and conjectures.
I don't know, but conversations of a spaced-out nature are
not uncommon. Having said this, I must head downstairs and
take my 3 p.m. dose of lithium. Don't laugh; it works...most
of the time.

Some might consider fishing with my stepfather, Ken. He died a few years back, but right up until the end he was in prime form, never missing an opportunity to give me or anyone else a bit of good-natured grief. Miss a fish and you'd hear about it in the most discreet yet biting of ways. Bring a nice one to net and you'd hear about that, too. Why did it take so long? Am I trying to exhaust the trout into a premature death?

Around 1990, he and I visited Dillon for a few days of fishing with Reiser. We spent a day each on the Beaverhead, Clark Canyon Reservoir, and the Big Hole. The late-summer weather was uncommonly hot, and the fish were down, but the three of us still managed to enjoy ourselves. With long days on the water, then long meals amid the cozy ambiance of the Bannack House, we survived.

By the time of this trip, age and a youthful bout with polio had slowed Ken down some. So, on the first day at Clark Canyon, Reiser left me to my own devices (a move of stunning courage on his part) and spent his time with my step-father. We were using float tubes, something Ken had never tried. As anyone who has used the devices can attest, the first time or two can be a curious and unique experience. I paddled off to some dead brush out from shore and began casting nymphs to the cover, all the while watching Reiser deal with the novitiate. To say that the scene had elements of confusion and awkwardness would be a mild understatement. Watching the guide help Ken into the tube, what with his fins flapping on the ground and in the water and that final graceful landing in the seat (the previously mentioned watermelon comes to mind), was almost as good as taking in a scintillating episode of the Tonight Show with Jay Leno, though topping this type of sophisticated comedy is out of reach for most of us mere mortals. Reiser and Ken paddled side by side to a likely looking spot and began casting.

Working a fly line from water level is an acquired skill (some might say an acquired taste), but Reiser persevered and soon Ken was fast into a nice fish, his rod arcing below the surface of the lake as the rainbow flashed hard silver 30 feet away. Clark Canyon's trout grow fast and large, and this one was no exception. Reiser moved in to net the tiring fish, but just as he made his move, so did the rainbow, diving down between Ken's legs and streaking off behind him. Line and obscenities were flying everywhere as he tried to turn around and deal with the crazed fish in a civilized manner. This never happened, but Ken did gain enough line to bring the trout close enough behind him for Reiser to bring the net into play. The trout was a solid 20 inches, and I would have hocked my inconsiderable fortune for a camera. Ken was pleased, glowing with a goofy grin on his face that appeared to say, "That's how it's done." Reiser gave up trying to control himself and cracked up. They both did. The nefarious duo spent the rest of the day fishing together, getting along famously. Reiser even managed to fool a wily carp with a hare's ear nymph. A tough, bruising fish that would put a brown to shame and embarrassed the hell out of the guide. The wind eventually came up, building whitecaps that sent spray flying east bound. We got off the water in the interests of safety and ingrained laziness and drove over to a pretty spring creek near town to watch some even prettier rainbows feed with refined delicacy on small mayflies. Then off to dinner. Another good day in southwest Montana, and Reiser showed me that his clients were more than a paycheck. He really enjoyed teaching people about flyfishing and definitely shared in their adventures.

Early on, I spent a lot of time with guides who cared little for the traditions and inherent beauty of chasing trout, and even less about the needs and desires of their clients, clients who seemed nothing more than pieces of meat to be run down a river, loaded up, carted back to a fly shop, and then relieved of fairly large sums of money. As the years passed, I discovered that this was not really the case, even back in those primitive '60s. Good guides and outfitters approach their work like professionals who enjoyed their craft—like Reiser. The others are mercenary losers. The percentage of these unenjoyable individuals has diminished over the years as anglers have grown in knowledge and expectations, but there are still enough of these hideous clowns ripping off the public that tales of miserable outings, abusive behavior, and shoddy treatment still surface with ugly regularity. I will never fish with anyone like this more than once. A friend of mine got so pissed off at one guide of this ilk that he jumped ship and walked to the nearest bar, which was several miles away. No easy task in neoprenes on a hot, sunny day. The guides I'm fortunate to know and fish with are all friends, patient, understanding, fun-loving souls with a sufficient collection of eccentricities to keep life interesting. The worst ones are the idiots who think they are God's gift to flyfishing and nothing a client can do is acceptable. In my frequently befuddled case this is frequently the situation, but I don't need to hear about it constantly in snide terms. Some of these guys think they're so damn good, that I doubt that A.J. McClane or Lee Wulff could have passed their ill-formed standards. May the in-it-for-a-buck, hustle-the-guy's-wife, I-know-more than you-ever-will bozos crash and burn beneath some mid-stream log jam. As it should be.

The next day we headed off to the Big Hole, about 30 minutes northwest of Dillon. Again a very hot, clear day. We put in and Reiser immediately spotted a school of good-sized browns working in the shallows. He quietly floated below them and let me off. I crept up on the fish with extreme stealth (stumbling over rocks and scaring off a heron); yet, after peeking around a boulder I saw that the browns were still feeding. I measured the cast to the lowest one and managed to put a slight curve in the presentation. The dry floated right into the fish's lane and he took. I set like a tuna boat crewman and was rewarded with a sharp "ping." Snapped tippet. Lost fish. The trout fled for cover and sanity. The others were spooked and fed erratically. Two quick sloppy casts put them down. A healthy morning's work in the space of 15 minutes.

"Nice job, John," Ken offered while chewing on a Claro corona that smoked with sublime intent.

"Never seen a pod fished that well before, Holt," added Reiser. "Keep it up. This could be the day of a lifetime."

I climbed aboard muttering something of a cheerful nature.

Reiser pulled over at the head of a long, deep run that boiled and shoved the water into choppy froth. I grabbed my camera and walked to the tail of the riffle hoping to catch Ken at the peak of his form, which I did. Rounding the bend I watched as Reiser frantically pulled on the oars against the current, trying vainly to maneuver into calm water. My stepfather was fast into a rainbow that jumped like crazy, then appeared to be drowning as it was dragged through the swift current. An image of The Wreck of the Mary Deare popped into my head. In truth, Ken was an excellent fisherman, but had not spent much time dealing with things from a moving craft, but I got my photos: Ken playing/dragging the trout; Ken smiling as he held the fish in the water; Ken reviving the fish; and finally, thank God, Ken releasing the rejuvenated rainbow. A pictorial essay that only the extremely bored or polite family members would find to be of any interest. Flyfishing is a highly personal, spontaneous experience best shared among those that were there. Reading about these sorts of things or looking at photographs can give a person an idea of the mayhem, but it's hard to feel the cold water, smell the pine in the air, and feel the sun or the strength of a wild fish while reading a book (Holt, do you realize what you just said?).

Temperatures closed in on 100 degrees by afternoon and the fishing was nonexistent as it was too hot and way too bright. The sun beat down hammering us into lethargic submission. We made half-hearted attempts at casting: lazy flicks of the rod that rippled the lines and bedraggled flies a few feet closer to the slowly passing banks. Far above us in the crumbling rock cliffs a band of some sort of ungulate clattered along, sending streams of stones sliding down to the near dead river. Conversation waned, then stopped entirely. The three of us were alone with our thoughts lost in somnolent daydreams. This is a common occurrence on the water, whether it is caused by the heat, fishing in the doldrums, an icy storm, or just temporary lassitude. The reason doesn't matter, it just happens.

Reiser was familiar with the malady and made no attempt at sprightly conversation. He wasn't being rude or not performing his job; he simply realized that neither of us were up for conversation. Sure, it's nice to catch trout on every cast, but that can turn boring and routine. Part of being on the river, is *being* on the river, sinking into its rhythms and patient pace. Constant action requires concentration, and before you know it the day is over and you don't really have an overall sense of the river you just floated. While several miles of this may sound deadly, I find myself recalling countless images of the landscape during this lull: those cliffs; the oil slick surface of the river reflecting the blue of the sky; eagles wheeling far overhead, their sharp cries sounding lonely, distant, from another country. I can still feel the dry heat. And I remember looking ahead at Ken somewhat slumped down, idly mending his line and staring at the water. It's all part of fishing, actually a fine memory in an odd sort of way, one that would have been ruined by a gabby guide.

Toward evening, as dusk settled around us, some browns started working on emerging caddis. We all caught some of them   fish to 18 inches—made more exciting by the low-intensity spell earlier. Another great day on the river.

On the last day, we worked the Beaverhead. It was hot again, but with clouds moving in, the air was damp with the coming precipitation. You could smell the willows and the richness of the river. We caught rainbows and browns steadily. I broke off a large fish. Ken took one of 20 inches, and Tollet nymphed four nice rainbows and a whitefish now and then. By the third day, a routine had been established among us and the atmosphere was long past guide and clients; more like three old fishing buddies doing what they liked best. A good guide creates this mood with nearly unconscious ease and it makes a fun trip special.

Near the take-out, a horrendous storm packed with lightning, hail, and pelting rain drenched us. The electricity-charged ozone was thick on the air, tingling along my arms. Pyrotechnics like this scare the hell out of me on the water or when I'm out bird hunting in exposed country. Thankfully, we pulled off the river and safely waited out the event. Almost as soon as the storm stopped, a blizzard hatch of caddis blanketed the river. Trout were everywhere, big and little. Our imitations were lost among the millions of whirling bugs. Our lines and flies knocked down the caddis when we cast.

Just as the Interstate bridge and the take-out came into view, a very large brown slammed Ken's fly. The brown rattled the water and ran back and forth, but Ken held on and the trout finally tired. The fish lay on its side next to the raft. Reiser measured it at 22 inches—one of the largest of my stepfather's life.

We were all grinning like fools.

"Ken, I guess this one's worth an extra Bombay double martini," Reiser suggested expectantly.

"If you're buying," Ken replied without missing a beat.

"I was afraid of that."

An appropriate ending to a damn nice trip.

Like I said, they're all crazy in Dillon, and I hope they never find the cure.

E·I·G·H·T

Ship of Fools

LULU WAS HAVING A RIOT. She was a one-woman mixture of equal parts enthusiasm, lunacy, laughter, good nature, and athleticism, and the fact that she was gorgeous didn't hurt either. She was six feet tall, well proportioned, and a redhead. (Hell, they're all redheads if you look at things a certain way.) Just another one passing, as swiftly through my life as we were running through this wild valley, on an untamed river with a mind of its own.

Lulu was catching cutthroats on nearly every cast, beautiful little silvery trout that hit the elk hair caddis with the enthusiasm of a kid on the first day of his first job. The trout would streak up from the bottom and nail the fly then put up a gallant fight full of head shakings and brief circular dashes. We released them all, but would keep several later for dinner. For someone who had never flyfished before, my companion was doing okay; she was a natural, not intimidated by the line or the rhythm needed to cast line with accuracy to seams and pockets. Most impressive was that she didn't yell and scream at every take. Sure she was excited—the smile, glint in her eyes and the quick yet controlled movements said as much—but she displayed a degree of casual joy with each cutthroat caught and returned to the river that was nice to see. And she insisted,

I mean insisted, that she slip the fish free from the hold of the hook.

We had about 60 miles of river to float and had allowed at least four days to cover the distance. I'd borrowed the raft from a trusting friend who said he didn't need it for at least a week, so we were safe at home on that count. I could row the thing well enough, so that I figured we had at least a 50/50 chance of surviving the trip. The weather was ideal for early August— low 80s, a light breeze, and a few puffy clouds coasting by above us. The river was running clear, sapphire, and at normal summer levels. I didn't even think we'd need a tent. Aside from caddis, stoneflies, mayflies, and hoppers, there were no bugs to speak of. There was the occasional deerfly, but no mosquitoes.

We were adequately provisioned and if the whole thing took an extra day or two, that was no big deal either; time was on our side for a change. My sister was taking care of my golden, Zachery, and Bouchee, the crazed springer spaniel, was holding court in the rear seat. The two-year-old dog was sitting on his haunches and leaning against the seat back, head slowly turning from side to side, creating an illusion of a king taking in his surroundings while his faithful servant chauffeured him through his domain. I knew better, but a nice try all the same.

I'd met Lulu a few years earlier while having a couple of drinks at the Old Faithful Bar in Gallatin Gateway: a great place with a superb collection of old rodeo photographs hanging from the walls; warped wooden floors; dusty windows; honest drinks. I'd just finished signing a bunch of books for a publisher who lived nearby, and of course could never pass up the chance to stop in at the tavern. Lulu was with a film production crew that was shooting location shots for some Hollywood extravaganza. Some of them decided to kill a few hours shooting pool and drinking at the Old Faithful, and I struck up a casual conversation in my own smooth way when she came to the bar to order another round for her and her friends. Turned out she was interested in the idea of flyfishing, no doubt hypnotized by the movie based on that Norman

Maclean novella. She delivered the drinks and returned to sit on a stool next to me. We talked a lot about fishing and a bunch of other stuff for a few hours, then I climbed off my perch, told her to look me up if she was ever in the Whitefish area, and handed her a ragged business card. I had about 30,000 of the things and had handed out maybe four in the last eight years. Realizing that an extended bout of driving was out of the question, I checked in (or out) at a motel a few miles down the road and fell asleep watching rugby on ESPN.

The next morning I drove home having totally forgotten about the previous night's conversation. But a couple of summers later the phone rang and it was Lulu. I had trouble placing her at first, then it all came to me like a '60s-inspired flashback. She asked if the invitation for fishing was still good. Could she come and visit for awhile? When you live in Montana, and if you happen to be a generous soul after a few drinks, this kind of thing happens a lot. Even if you don't invite people, they still come—cousins, friends you haven't heard from since the last time they needed bail money, a magazine editor that butchered your copy more than once, almost anyone—and will call and ask if they can come out and visit. I even had a guy who worked for a group of car dealerships in Wichita and his friend, a circuit court judge, call and ask to visit. They did and we had an interesting and fine time, but they only knew me prior to their expedition from reading my books, and I only knew them from a couple of phone conversations. They were brave souls and they'll be back. That's how it is sometimes, and I love it. You never know who will show up at the front door in a rental (or stolen) car or what the next few days will bring. Freeform recreation at Lake Holt Inn.

Anyway, I figured that I had nothing to lose, and I wasn't busy at the moment "Are you working or just writing?" I've been queried all too often. People figure that if you make a semblance of a living from tapping a keyboard, instead of getting dirt under your nails, foreclosing on mortgages, planning housing developments for open spaces or playing professional sports (Go Deion), you just ain't doing anything. You get used to it, and I laugh every morning when I wake up and decide whether to "work," go fishing, or just sit in the sun and play with the dogs. So I told Lulu to come on up. I'd meet her at Kalispell International Airport (the European concourse is on the far right of the complex). She offered to pay whatever the going rate was for guiding, and any other incidental expense. I figured that since there was a reasonable chance that I'd manage to swamp the raft and drown both of us in the process, I'd wave my customary fee of $5 per day. We'd split the cost of food, beverages, and gas. All she had to bring was clothes, a little money, and herself. I had enough flyfishing and camping gear to outfit several large expeditions. No money, but an awful lot of fly rods and reels.

The jet arrived on time and scads of confused tourists disembarked—well over 100 goofballs dressed in black, skin-tight stretch pants, tons of make-up, flashy gold jewelry, and garish lamé tops. Half of them were men, I think. Where's my gun?

Lulu was last off the plane, a trait we had in common. She was wearing jeans, a faded blue dress shirt (button-down collar), and worn, white Converse All Star low-cuts. I looked at her, then at myself. We were dressed alike except she looked a hell of a lot better and had a hell of a lot more hair.

"John," she said, and rushed up and gave me a hug. (Remember, I'd seen her just once before.) "I've missed you so much. Let me look at you." Oh Jesus, this is going to be a long gig, I thought.

"Drop the crap, Lulu. We don't even know each other."

"John. You cut me to the quick," and she really did look hurt. "After all, we've had drinks together. I'm just giving you some LA shit like I'm sure you expected. Let's get the hell out of here. I can't stand these people. Southern California. What a wasteland. And I live there. God. I hope they don't ruin Montana like they've dumped on Arizona and other places. Vermin."

"They're doing their best, Lulu, but don't get me started. I left the Beretta at home. Where's your bag?"

"This is it," and she lifted an old, and I mean really battered, Orvis Battenkill duffel bag she had somehow managed to get on the plane. It was covered with duct tape and would never make the catalog. "This thing has been everywhere. If it could only talk."

"I'd like to hear what it has to say," I said, while damn near throwing my back out lifting it. "What the hell's in here? Hard drugs?"

"You should be so lucky. Clothes and books. I plan to read some while I float. You write the silly things, so you should be supportive of me on this, John."

I shrugged and dragged the duffel off to the portable death trap—my 1984 Toyota pickup—rusty, battered rig that I'll keep forever. The tape player is long gone, the heater barely works, and the driver's window operates by pulling it up by hand. Brakes, engine, and wipers are good, though. Two Chicago Cubs stickers adorn the bumper and a large round of Doug fir makes do as snow tires in the winter. The truck is all I need or want. Screw the yupsters driving around Whitefish in their really neat Ford Explorers, Range Rovers, BMWs, and Cadillac Sevilles. Lulu grabbed the duffel and swung it into the back with ease. I was impressed and she winked with a sly grin. She hopped in the truck with a sincere sounding "nice rig," and we were off wheeling and dealing with the others as we tried to funnel through the tollgate and out to the freedom of the open road. We pulled in front of my place in the space of a lukewarm beer. Bouchee and Zack leapt all over Lulu, and the three of them barked, moaned, and whined for long minutes, soon becoming fast friends though communicating on a level I wasn't sure I wanted any part of. Before dinner we went shopping for food and booze and a few odds and ends, then loaded everything, in the back of the truck. We'd take the truck and a friend's old beater Chevy half-ton that he didn't need for awhile (like forever) to run the shuttle. We were set and finished off the night with a touch of cognac and some Punch double maduro cigars. Lulu was alright. To tell the truth I didn't have many female friends who shared my excellent tastes in clothes, trucks, food, cigars, and booze. I wondered if she could row.

We left early the next morning and were on the water by nine.

"Time for lunch, Lulu."

"You mean beer, don't you, John?"

The space behind the rowing platform was filled with coolers (in addition to the one I was sitting on) and dry bags filled with food (including a five-pound bag of Purina for Bouchee), beer, pop, liquor, clothes, and camping gear. With these fish, all this fresh water and a little foraging, we could hang out on the river until late fall. The raft glided into a small bay with a sand and stone shore. I tossed a few cushions out and dragged the lunch cooler on shore. Lulu blew a lot of money on our food, as she planned on doing most of the cooking. She bought top-shelf, quality stuff, so I went into this knowing that at least we wouldn't starve. I cracked open a couple of Schmidts (I bought a case to bug her), and we dined graciously on smoked lamb and Bermuda onion on sourdough bread sandwiches, corn chips with avocado and jalapeño pepper dip, red grapes, and some sharp, white cheddar cheese. One more beer and it was nap time for this boy. There was a nice spot to camp three miles downstream, two easy hours from here even with some stops to fish a couple of deep pools. But that would be later, as the last thing I heard was me snoring.

Ever since my most recent divorce (I'm only up to two), I've been having vivid though bizarre, weird, psychotic dreams. They have reached such a high level of verisimilitude that I frequently have trouble telling apart what most of us consider reality from some dream episodes. I've dreamed that, while wearing a jousting outfit and riding a coal-black stallion, I rode down the Pillsbury Doughboy, hopped off the steed and punched out the perfectly-browned, fresh-from-the-oven, lightly-buttered little fella. I've dreamed, and this one is scary, that I woke up one Sunday morning with Martha Stewart lying in bed next to me and that, while making love, we also had a pleasant conversation about pruning roses. I also dreamed that I was sitting in the leftfield bleachers and caught the ball Ernie

Banks hit for a championship-winning homerun in the bottom of the ninth. These are the dreams I'm willing to admit to. Others will never see the light of print. Never.

I don't have the abilities required to be a good guide, nor do I want to be a guide. Dealing with the human race in a sensible and civilized fashion is not one of my priorities. But I do spend some time thinking about what they must go through to make ends meet. The dream I had following lunch that first day on the river with Lulu probably reflects this.

I'd been floating down a classic trout stream in Montana (I knew intuitively it was in Montana) with my clients who were in their early 40s and of intermediate ability. They were dressed to the nines in many hundreds of dollars of fancy clothing—designer neoprenes, teal colored vests, wildly colored fishing shirts with dozens of pockets, top-of-the-line rods, Wheatley fly boxes, 700-dollar reels—the whole sad routine. The rainbows were in fine form, and the pair caught trout after trout on blue-winged olive chutes. Big fish to 20 inches—strong, acrobatic, intensely colored. Every time they netted one of these marvelous creatures each would say, "Nice fish." They pretended to be happy with each other's success but they were also keeping score. "That makes 31." "I think I've caught at least 40 and one was 24 inches."

They treated me politely but with a manner that clearly said I was nothing more than a poorly-educated lout in their employ, and I should be damn happy about it. This is a skill I've noticed that yupster subnormals, who have made a killing by screwing their partner, family, friends, and unrelated victims out of every cent they had, seemed to have acquired at birth. They owned the most expensive of everything without appreciating its value. They flyfished, as they did all else, because it was the thing to do. They only read the flyfishing magazine that spoke to them, the one that patterned itself after *Outside*. Sort of a flyfishing version of *Town and Country* and *Cosmopolitan*. You know the one I mean.

Anyway, I was beginning to lose it, and a few nips from a flask of bourbon were not enough. Finally, when the husband, lord, arbitrageur, or whatever, landed a 20-plus rainbow, ripped it from the hook, and flung it disdainfully back into the river with a sickening splash, I'd had enough. I stood up, turned around, and decked the sucker with a freeform right hook that came in like an overdue freight train. I felt his jaw tear and shatter as he went overboard. Then I addressed the feminine fool in the bow, who I took mercy on by merely grabbing her and tossing her overboard. Laughing, I drained my flask, opened a beer, lit a cigar, and rowed away. The hell with 'em. Onward and upward.

I didn't hear anything about the incident until a fellow guide came to my front door with a summons in his hand. Apparently, another guide wanted me outlawed from the profession, and my presence was requested at the annual guides and outfitters adjudication gathering at a large, ancient ponderosa pine that grew on the Rocky Mountain Front along the Sun River. By the way, this was always held on April Fool's Day. So I drove over.

There were hundreds of men and women there—guides and outfitters all from Montana. Tents were everywhere, with fires burning in front of each—quite a friendly, sociable gathering with drinking and merrymaking. My case was to be the third of the morning, and I enlisted a guide friend from the Bitterroot to defend me. The judge was a fly shop owner of venal disposition. The guide who brought suit against me was a Bighorn player. I was in deep shit; neither one of these guys liked me in the least. Actually, they hated my guts. The feeling was mutual. When my case was called, the charges of indecent treatment of clients who were more than willing to overpay and tip generously were detailed. I recounted the day's events that led to my actions. The Bozeman-based judge took five seconds to reach a decision. I was to be outlawed for six years, banished to guiding on the Little Missouri in the southeastern corner of the state over by the town of Olive, population four. In addition, I was to be tied to the ponderosa and whipped one dozen times with an Orvis Trident "stealth technology" 9-weight, 9-foot fly rod. So, three of my peers dragged me to the old tree and lashed me firmly to its trunk using 30-pound dacron backing that was cinched so tightly my skin tore. The Bighorn guide, a tall, mangy, hideous-looking specimen who was only in it for a buck, picked up the rod, flexing the wand in his gnarled right hand. I closed my eyes. I heard the swish of the rod as it ripped through the air, felt the biting sting as it struck...

"Ahhhhhhh. Damn." I sat up in a cold sweat. Where's Martha? Where's the doughboy? This has got to stop. Maybe I should witness at a TU meeting next month."

"What in the hell is going on? You've been moaning and swearing off and on since you nodded off," asked Lulu with a smile that also betrayed concern and a pinch of bewilderment. "Jesus, boy. You got some demons working away inside you. Grab a beer. No. Make that two and let's shove off and tag some of those pretty cutthroat. I'll even row. Looks pretty tame for the next mile from what I can see." I didn't argue. Episodic dreams were proving to be a draining experience.

Lulu pulled us smartly out into the current and then worked us toward a long run below a tall gravel cutbank. Pines lay tops down, like dead soldiers, on the steep slope, victims of erosion from runoff flooding earlier in the year. She kept the raft about 30 feet from shore, bow first, holding position by pulling back on the oars with even, steady strokes. I was amazed. Had she been a guide in a previous incarnation? Was she one now? I was fishing a #12 brown elk hair with a gray dubbed body and a cream hackle, one of my favorite patterns in this part of Montana, in southern British Columbia, and Alberta. Big and little trout love the thing. I've caught fish from 4 to 24 inches on the fly tied in sizes ranging from 8 to 18. It has replaced the ubiquitous Adams as my universal bug of choice.

The run was about a mile long, curving in an extended oxbow. To the east, totally undisciplined mountains staggered far into the sky, peaks ragged and busted up from past glaciation. Snow and ice clung to their flanks. A rich forest of larch, glowing bright green rolled up to the base of the cliffs. Native grass meadows carpeted the ground to the edge of the banks, and roots from the plants dangled in the air over the water. Deer browsed lazily, sometimes lifting their heads to stare at us as we passed. The elk hair took fish after fish, and when cast in the deep seam a foot from the bank, the cutthroats would literally fight for the fly, two and three at a time. In that lengthy drift I caught eight or nine fish to 14 inches. Could have been more, but I was slow on releasing the fish and getting the pattern back on the water. Lulu held position perfectly with the bow angled slightly into the bank, making all of this almost too easy. Perfect.

"You've done this before?"

"I did a little guiding in the Canyon and rowed some for a couple of movies we filmed on the Gunnison, but this is the first time in a long time," she said while wiping a few beads of sweat from her forehead.

"No complaints here. You're doing so well you might as well take us in to camp. It's only a couple of miles and there's just one narrow chute to cope with."

"Thought you'd pull something like this, but what the heck. This is fun."

The scenery stayed outrageous. This is overthrust country, the valley developing when the earth's crust stretched after the overthrust belt formed. It contains a deep fill of basin sediments often called the Kishenehn formation, even though they appear to be the same as the Renova formation (formed during the Oligocene and early Miocene periods that includes an assortment of gravel, sand, mud, volcanic ash, limestone, and coal as much as 2,000 feet thick) of other western Montana valleys. Deep deposits of glacial debris blanket most of the floor, making exposures of the older fill hard to locate. Early settlers noticed that they could recognize bear skins from this valley because they smelled like kerosene. They solved that mystery in the 1890s by finding several oil seeps that the creatures liked to wallow in. Several wells since that time have turned up indications of gas and oil, but fortunately, no one is drilling commercially. Yet.

"John, how do you know this stuff?"

"I read books, Lulu. And a couple of decades ago that was one of my many minors in one of the many colleges I went to."

"Just not educational material, were you? I'm not surprised. You were probably one of those drug-crazed hipsters my mother warned me about. You probably even listened to the Mothers of Invention."

"I have all their records and all of Bonzo Dog's, too."

"'Tubas in the Moonlight?'"

"Of course."

"You're sick."

"I try my best, and anyone who knows that song has to be twisted herself."

"Well, I am in my 40s and I did see the band in Belfast in the early '70s. They came out on stage wearing Budweiser boxing shorts and gas masks and opened with Tubas."

"They just don't have quality music like that these days."

"Waxing soporific on me, John. Not a good sign. Better kill a brace or two of those cutthroat for dinner."

This was easily done, with six casts and six pan-sized trout for dinner. I have no qualms about taking a few fish for dinner every now and then. Absolute adherence to catch and release is anathema to flyfishing, which, after all, is a blood sport—yupsters and posy fuckers be damned. They would taste great sautéed in butter and wine with a little salt and pepper. And Lulu bought an exotic variety of wines, one I'm sure would match nicely with the trout. A tossed salad and some wild rice —maybe a little Brie beforehand, cigars, and cognac afterward while babbling around a fire as evening settled in: brutal trip. This one was turning rough.

The spot we picked to spend the night was one of my favorites. A long, wide expanse of sand next to the river. Thick pine forest behind and a view of the mountains stretching from far in the south all the way into British Columbia. There was an excellent riffle and pool to fish, plenty of dry wood and no bugs. We lay our sleeping bags on top of a large tarp, unloaded eight tons of food stuffs, and built a fire. The day, even past seven, was still warm. We built drinks and collapsed in the sand to watch the fire burn down to a bed of cooking coals. I did the fish, while the rice soaked in a pot and Lulu took care of the salad. A couple of bottles of Chablis from a French vineyard I'd never heard of were on ice. A round of Brie and some decent crackers even made an appearance. I was getting embarrassed at the dining opulence, yet relaxed from the day spent outside. So was my companion. In the space of 24 hours we'd become fishing buddies, friends. Sometimes that's the way things turn out, but I've experienced the other end of the spectrum, times when things turned bleak and ugly. Like the trip with a fool from Denver who turned out to be an argumentative whiner and a wimp. I ditched him in Dillon at a motel and haven't seen him since. I don't know what happened to him, nor do I care. This trip with Lulu was far different and obviously much better.

"John, ever think of guiding for a living?" Lulu said. She sipped her Margarita, a drink made from fresh limes, true Mescal, and real sea salt. Like I said, top shelf all the way. I worked on some Jack Daniel's on the rocks.

"No way. I'm not all that good rowing a raft, and at best I'm an average fisherman. And my social skills, especially when dealing with assholes, are somewhat deficient. Too much pressure, too much work. I'll let those who enjoy it and know what they're doing take care of business. The way you row and with your looks, if you don't mind a compliment, you wouldn't need to know Jack shit about flyfishing to earn a living. A woman friend of mine just moved to Whitefish and is doing okay guiding, though she's been fishing for years. She says the tips keep tumbling her way, in somewhat direct proportion to the amount of clothing she has on. Hot weather, halter tops, and short cutoffs. More money."

"Are you one of those awful Montana sexists I've heard so much about?"

"Yes."

"Honest about it, anyway. No. I'm like you. The way we're doing the river is the way it should be for antisocial people like us. Crowds bother me, make me nervous, that's why I live in la-la land. More than three people and I get confused." Lulu made us each another drink while I put the cast-iron frying pan on the grill over the embers along with the rice.

Dinner was ready in about another half hour and eaten in less than five minutes. We cleaned up the mess, threw a bunch of wood on the fire, dragged out the Cognac and a couple of Hoya de Monterrey Excalibur No. 2s in natural wrappers, lighted up, and reclined on our sleeping bags, duffels for bench rests: heaven as dusk turned to night. The aroma of the cognac and cigars blended perfectly with that of the river and the pines, yet you could never bottle this fragrance. Stars were coming out and the tips of our cigars were miniature suns glowing hot-orange in the dark. We smoked and sipped the wine in silence. No talk, just the sound of the river flowing over the rocky streambed, the hissing of burning cigars and the infrequent howl of coyotes (or wolves?). Hours passed and I woke up as the sun was making a bid to clear the mountains. Dew was on the sleeping bags and Lulu was curled up next to me for warmth. I got up and rebuilt the fire and made coffee. The older I get, the stiffer I am in the morning, and throughout the rest of the day for that matter. I can't even remember what it felt like to be 20. But having this attractive woman asleep in my camp with a wild river rolling by had its compensations.

I walked down to the river with a mug of very strong, black coffee and watched as westslope cutthroat worked steadily along an inside ribbon of current feeding easily on emerging mayflies. The cutts and bull trout, along with mountain whitefish, are native to this river. The first two species are threatened from sedimentation from clearcutting along their spawning streams and from loss of habitat due to development. In fact, you can no longer legally fish for the bulls because their numbers have dropped so low. Will the cutthroat be next? I prefer fishing for native species, anytime; there's something about catching trout that have evolved to fill a certain niche in an ecosystem. Cutthroat are not hard to fool in these waters and they are beautiful, wild fish. Bull trout, on the other hand, require sinking lines and large, weighted streamers. They grow to over 20 pounds and hold tight in deep runs and huge pools. They love the shelter of logjams, too.

Following a leisurely breakfast, we got on the water a little after 10. I packed the raft while Lulu took a dip in the brisk water. (I'd wait until the afternoon when the sun had warmed things up some.) I rigged up an 8-weight with a teeny sink-tip line and a 7-foot leader with an 0X tippet. To this, I tied on a large red and white streamer of my own design: Marabou, dyed fur, lead, mylar, all secured to a long-shanked 1/0 hook. After Lulu dressed, I let her practice on shore with the ungainly out-fit. The first few attempts were fraught with eye-piercing danger, but she soon picked up on the needed hesitation in the back cast to allow the rod to load and the firm shoot on the forward stroke. She really was a natural. I explained where I thought the best spots for the bulls would be and off we went. I really wanted to see her face when she hooked a 10-pounder, which were definitely in the river at this time of year.

She worked several runs and pools thoroughly without even a bump, which made me wonder if the fish had keyed on the water temperature of their native tributaries and dashed far upstream into the wilderness. We stopped at a large pool about 100 yards below a creek that supported a decent run of bulls, and on about the third cast, her rod jerked straight down into the river. I saw a whitish flash on the bottom at the take. Lulu reared back on the rod and set the hook with three quick pumps. The bull rattled its head and started a determined run downstream toward a jumble of gray, dead limbs and tree trunks. Lulu went right after the fish without my advice and even tightened down on the drag as she negotiated the rocky shoreline. She had a chance but needed to check the fish before it reached the current feeding into the jam. About 50 yards out the fish rolled on the surface, and Lulu walked onto shore and slowly pulled back on the rod, now bowed into the classic art. The fish stopped, then came toward shore with increasing speed. Lulu reeled like crazy and moved back again, regaining control. The fish, easily 10 pounds, ran back and forth in the sandy shallows and was tiring rapidly. I moved in slowly behind it. I could hear Lulu breathing heavily with exertion and excitement, while her face was flushed and her eyes were wide open, sparkling, the pupils pinned. She had the look, and I knew it well. Finally, the fish turned on its side and I grabbed its tail with both hands. Large, well-defined kype, dark aquamarine coloring with bright orange spots, pink tinting along the lower flanks and belly. Orange fins tipped with white and black. Rows of wicked teeth: a bull trout. Lulu dropped the rod and splashed toward me.

"God damn. Look at that. Beautiful. Absolutely beautiful," she whispered. "You weren't kidding about these guys. I can see why you're addicted. Let me touch him."

"Here, it's your fish. Hold him. Feel how heavy this one is."

She did, cradling the salmonid ahead of the tail and just behind the head. She looked up at me with the grin, then turned the fish around, slowly revived it and turned the bull loose in the gentle current. The wonderful fish swam off into the river, fading slowly from view.

"As they say, the sun is over the yardarm somewhere. Let's crack a bottle of champagne," and she was off rooting around in one of the coolers. I watched the river and hoped that these fish would be here forever. I heard a loud pop and a cork came flying my way. Turning I saw Lulu upending the bottle, the wine pouring down her chin and coming out her nose.

"Class act, Lulu. When it starts squirting out your ears, you're full. Give me some of that."

And that's how the next few days went. Plenty of action for cutthroat on top and a couple of more smaller bull trout below. Fine weather, grand country, and pleasant company. Then the trip was over and Lulu was boarding a jet all too soon, but she said she'd be back again. I hoped so. If they were all like her, I could see guiding. For free.

A few weeks later my cousin, Steve, and his wife, Emily, flew up from the madness of Denver for a long weekend. My friend, Jake, and the three of us floated the same river that Lulu and I had run earlier. For late in the summer it was hot, in the 80s or more down in the canyons with the heat bouncing around the rock and off the water's smooth surface. Jake rowed most of the time, though Steve gave it a try near the end, finally getting the hang of rowing against, and not with, the current. We caught countless small cutthroat, a smattering of rainbows and a couple of brook trout and whitefish. The day was made special by flat-out fantastic weather, and the four of us had a fine time. Any good day by mid-September in the northern Rockies feels like you have cheated the reaper, after a fashion. Winter's hiding over the mountains across the U.S.-Canadian border, waiting to swoop down and wail away on the Flathead Valley with a cold, windy intensity.

The float this day was only about eight miles, so we took our time, stopping here and there to work a promising-looking pool, wade in the still summer-warm water, or just bake on the hot rocks. A casual float with no expectations other than the promise of several stress-free, lazy hours, and that's what we got. We pulled off the river around five, returned home mildly cooked by the sun, showered, and went out to dinner in town, where we gorged on everything brought to our table, only to return home to annihilate a half-gallon of coffee-flavored ice cream and then totter off to dreamland. An average Montana day. I'll take as many as I can get.

The point of all of this is, if guiding was as easy as showing kind individuals like Lulu, Steve, or Emily a high time on area rivers and lakes, I'd be in the business in a heartbeat. But I know better. So does Jake. Weather, fish, strange people, weird regulations, jacked-up liability insurance rates—you name it—all conspire to make the life of a guide hell on earth at times. I don't have what it takes to do the profession justice. I can clearly see that.

I'll leave the hard, detail work to the pros. Besides I'd rather write than work any day.

N·I·N·E

Lost to the World

THERE REALLY ISN'T MUCH GOING ON here right now, but it's a damn nice day nevertheless, what with lots of blue sky, few clouds, warm temperatures, light breeze, and crystalline sunlight filtering through the cedars and pines. Damn nice river, too; fast flowing, clear aquamarine washing over a cobbled streambed. Mayflies and caddis hatching in some sort of natural rhythm and a few rainbows, cutthroat, and brook trout feeding with midsummer leisure. Cold hard times are way off in the distance, hiding up north behind the space of linear time. Frank Chance and I were anchored in midstream making marginal efforts at casting to the rising fish. Soft, sloppy casts, a few feet of elk hair, and the fish would take with eager, small splashes and slurps. All of them, even the silly cutts, would thrash and leap before coming to us. Nothing big, perhaps 14 inches tops, but all were wild, healthy trout. We released them all, and we finally gave in to sitting in the drift boat and sipping our beers and taking in the day. I think we'd been hard at this wicked behavior for a couple of hours, but time was essentially meaningless on the northwestern Montana river, on any good river for that matter. I looked back at Frank. Asleep at the wheel. Chin bobbing on his chest, a small rivulet of drool snaking from the corner of his mouth. A good man. Always on top of things. My kind of guide and friend.

I'd met Frank several years back after he called me out of the blue and asked if I wanted to hunt ruffed grouse in his country. Said he had a great little golden he called Sadie and a pretty lady companion who made the best margaritas on the planet. He was right on both counts; Sadie could hunt all day and Jane could make a fine drink and an even finer meal. Frank and I even hit a bird apiece during my all too brief stay. I'd found another piece of heaven hiding from the rapacious development maniacs and made three fine friends in the process. It was as good a four days as I've ever spent in early October. Hell, anytime. Open, generous individuals living an honest life in unspoiled country. All of it's going away in a hurry, but at least not here, not yet.

October in Montana is special. The light glows softly when the days are nice, and that's exactly what they are, nice. We'd wake a little after sunup, have coffee and rolls, and drive off into the woods in the mountains surrounding the small, comfortable cabin they lived in beside the river. Days warmed quickly, so we only hunted for a couple of hours, much to the disappointment of Sadie. She'd kick up the birds—grouse that dived and spun through the tree limbs—we'd shoulder our guns, make a lot of noise, and walk on under the reproachful glare of the golden. But Sadie wasn't one to get too upset; she just liked to give us a touch of grief when we missed easy shots. Most of the time it seemed, but the three of us had a high, old go of it; talking about the birds, the country, the environment, writers (Frank wrote, too; a shortcoming in some of us, but at least he did it well), trout. We were all over the place with our conversation—friends from the start. By midday we'd head for a sandwich at one of the bars scattered along the valley. Then we'd wander off to the river or maybe some small, delightful feeder creek that held native redband trout: pure, aboriginal relatives of the rainbows, glorious little fish of maybe eight to ten inches. The trout pounced on dries like Royal Wulffs or Adams. Fought a bit and tired. I would have loved to taste one cooked in a cast-iron pan with butter, lemon, salt, and pepper. But these fish are special, some of the last of their dying breed. In this case, fleshly delights take a back seat to survival of wild things.

The streams were all lined with pine, cedar, willow, alder, and aspen; yellow-gold and browning leaves swirled in the eddies our legs made as we worked our way upstream. A time of life and beauty made stronger the sense of approaching death that the coming winter brings in me. I love this intensity and am terrified by its truth. The fishing was easy: 20-foot casts at the most, upstream to tiny pools; little backwaters spinning behind rocks or along through small glides. The redbands were always there and willing. You'd see the red, green, and white fly bouncing along, then a colorful fish sweeping up from cover to hit the fly with a splashy take. Our 2-weights bent out of respect for the natives, and it was as fun to fish as it was when we were children. No big fish, longest cast bullshit—catching fish.

Later as the sun began to drop in the sky, we'd sidehill our way through some open stands of pine, the ground cover thick with huckleberry, beargrass, and juniper. The air was cool as it began to flow downhill, smelling of pine and the bare rock wall above us. The only sounds, other than those we made, were from ground squirrels skittering about, the croak of a raven or two, or the distant cry of an eagle or hawk. Sadie jumped more ruffed grouse for us, and one afternoon Frank hit one and on the next afternoon I dropped a bird. High skills surfacing in the northern Rockies. We could care less, as it was simply good being alive and wandering through this land.

By sundown we'd return to Frank's truck comfortably tired. Here we sat on the tailgate sipping beer and enjoying the last of the light. Then we'd head off to a tavern for a couple more beers and some casual talk with Frank's friends before heading back home for some tequila, a fine meal, and some animated conversation surrounded by good music. Frank, Jane, and Sadie had this number figured. A nice way to go.

One autumn a writer friend of mine from Vermont came over with me for some ruffed grouse. We stayed at Frank's, of course. We hooked up with another writer from the area, Dizzy Trout, who was talented, easy to smile, and with a little less hair than me. Dizzy was easy to like. His concern for the environment and what the fools were doing to destroy the land was equal to or greater than mine. Dizzy spent large chunks of time and a bit of his money writing extensive newsletters that he mailed to individuals around the country. He, along with Frank, wasn't about to roll over and watch the greedy bastards ruin their valley, even if they did have lots more money and power. Better to go down fighting than crying. In addition to all of his activities related to this country, Dizzy managed to find the time and energy to write damn good books, a number of them.

I have to admit that the notion of four writers wandering through the woods armed with various gauges of shotguns is a bit frightening, but aside from a couple of grouse, there were no casualties. More crisp fall weather, good talk, laughter, and smooth sailing in the mountains. Then another one of Jane's fine meals and midnight died a wicked death as did 1 a.m. and 2 a.m., and so on. We strung a few days of this together and even managed to scare up a flock of Canada geese that Frank and my Vermont friend fired at without incident.

I thought of moving to the valley, but was still married at the time, so I gave up on the concept, at least temporarily. Those days with Frank were the best part of our trip. Both my friend and I picked up some ruthless, exotic virus on the road somewhere between Lewistown and Glendive. Vodka helped some, but we were forced to hole up in a motel for several days in eastern Montana watching movies, eating starchy, greasy diner food, and trying not to drive each other crazy. We survived and my friend got his antelope out by Circle, but that's another story.

Another day, floating a large river that Frank's river empties into, we caught dozens of rainbows, and a few cutthroat, toward evening on PMDs. The fish were all over the smooth stretches of the stream, rise forms widening all around us. Cast just above a fish and he would take. Not large trout— 9 to 13 inches, maybe a little more—but strong silvery fish that made quick, slashing runs barely below the surface. We kept casting and catching trout into dark before pulling out and making our obligatory stop at a bar. By now, some of Frank's friends recognized me and readily included me in their talk, which seemed to weigh heavily on the side of critiquing my friend's angling and guiding skills.

"He's not charging for this, is he?" said an old logger with a face full of gray three-day-old whiskers. "Hell, only last week that half-assed boat of his sunk. Near drowned a couple from California. They got lucky and lived. Too bad 'bout that, though. And Keerist, ever see him cast? Great God Almighty. It's somethin' that he still has both his eyes. And I'll be damned how he's missed tagging that woman of his with those big bugs he throws. Luck must be with her."

"It didn't sink, we took in some water going through that chute above the falls, that's all," laughed Frank as he worked on a Rainier. "The river's too small to drown in, anyway."

"Not with you rowing, it ain't. Must be desperate for work if you're takin' that sorry excuse for a fisherman with you. What's he payin'?"

"Nothing. He's a friend. A writer from Whitefish."

"Jesus. Not another one. Too many here already. Not one of them worth a tinker's damn, either. And from that town. Nothing but an overgrown whorehouse for tourists."

Sometimes the truth makes you laugh even when it hurts, and I bought a round.

"Thanks for the drink, but that don't change nothin'," the old guy said around his whiskey, and everyone was having a fine time now, turning on each other in a good-natured way. I liked these people. Plenty of give and take. Honest bullshit, if that makes any sense. Hell, the marriage was already dead. I was really thinking about moving here now.

This is not to suggest that everything in this secluded valley is all sweetness. There have been incidents, situations, that even now seem curious. Admittedly, these took place when I was practicing the high art of drinking two or three bottles of Jim Beam per day and eating codeine tablets like they were M&Ms. But they seemed real enough at the time and still strike at least a minor chord of verisimilitude even in today's clear air...

The day started off normally enough. A casual drive up a winding logging road through tall stands of Douglas fir and a couple of logging trucks almost reduced us to a fine paste of metal, rubber, and mangled flesh. Such are the vicissitudes of mountain driving. Frank skillfully wrenched his pickup down into the ditch both times and only small quantities of our beverages were lost. Had these happy, chance encounters happened on exposed stretches of the road, we would have died. Fishing for small cutthroat can be exhilarating.

Further up the road, we bounced through a clearcut in progress. Mangled trees, piles of wasteful slash, frantic skid cats, and the honest sound of chainsaws dominated the bucolic scene. Mud, piles of dirt, and the smell of ripped pines was everywhere. Almost through the carnage, a 200-foot tree crushed a few feet in front of us, sending dirt and rock into the already-chipped windshield. Frank slammed on the brakes, but we piled into the pine's quivering limbs anyway, cracking the already-cracked windshield a little bit more. Our beverages were sloshing on the floor and the third adrenalin rush of the day was upon us.

"Sorry about that," laughed a subnormal masquerading as a human. "Didn't see you coming. Have this cut up and you'll be on your way in a few minutes," and the gentle soul fired up a large Stihl saw. We backed up, muttering various imprecations, and got out and drank a cold Vitamin R each. Nothing like cold beer bubbling down one's throat to calm addled nerves.

"That was entertaining," I said.

"Entertaining, hell. That was close. Asshole almost got us," muttered Frank as he reached for another beer. He must have been really upset as he rarely has more than one before noon. "Lot of my friends are loggers. They have some sense and care at least a little for the woods, but these big company, out-of-state pricks are only in it for the money. The bastards really think the forest, or lack of it, looks better, like mowing the yard, after they've scalped a hillside. I'm starting to agree with you. The human race is a failed experiment."

"I knew you'd come around. Speaking of failed experiments, how's that clown Biff Dare doing? Still killing every fish he and his clients catch? Who'd fish with the guy, anyway?"

"Whacks trout heads on the side of his boat, then throws them on the floor. He manages to find people from back east or cities on the coast. They don't know any better and Dare doesn't give a damn. Heard he punched a hole in another guide's raft last week. A real piece of work. Maybe he'll die soon."

"I doubt it, Frank. Old farts like that live forever."

We finished our Rainier's, climbed back into the truck, and fled the carnage, happy we were not hurt and that the pickup still ran.

We found the tiny stream bubbling down the mountainside, pouring pure, ice cold. Moss-covered rocks lined the edges. Soft shades of green. I rigged up a one-ounce 2-weight and tied on a small elk hair—my favorite fly—one that always seems to work. Frank took the same route with his 2-weight. I walked downstream for 15 minutes, then stepped into the middle of the flow. I could feel the water coolness through my waders. Trout were snapping up bugs coming off in calm areas. A brief cast landed the fly above a small eddy, and a cutt took as soon as the pattern reached the swirl. The little guy danced on the surface, then came to me—eight inches of wild perfection, bright orange slashes along its jaw. I worked my way back to the truck catching fish on almost every cast. Frank showed up and we ate some grouse sandwiches on homemade whole wheat, some Gala apples, and a cold beer or two. The day's light played among the trees and scattered off the creek. Water rushing over the rocks played its sparkling tune. Nice place.

"Want you to meet some people I think you'll find interesting," said Frank, a slightly wicked grin was working across my friend's face. I knew good trouble was at hand. No bird hunting today. "They're in the middle of their annual autumn blow-out. Started a week ago. Should be up to speed by now. Doubt we'll get back tonight. Sadie will join us later."

"Who are these people?"

"Just some crazies that hang out up here. Great people. The usual collection of malcontents, societal dropouts, escaped felons, derelict writers. Your kind of crowd."

A few beers up the road, we pulled off into a large, grassy meadow filled with wildflowers, teepees decorated with sunbursts, goddesses, leaping trout, elk—the whole trip. A group of log cabins were clumped near the creek; the structures dilapidated, slowly crumbling back into the earth. There were lots of people resembling a '90s version of the crowd at the Rolling Stones' Altamont concert, the one where Hell's Angels, playing the part of the band's security force, killed some of the happy concertgoers. Long-haired hipsters, bikers, barebreasted women, the obligatory marauding bands of scruffy children, dogs of all description—I'd seen this scene once or twice before. Los Lobos' "Mas y mas" was blaring from large speakers mounted in ponderosa pines. Chaos—complete chaos. I'd have to adjust my world view as far as this valley was concerned.

We hopped out and Frank was soon out of sight, lost in the melee. A gnome with long red pigtails handed me a bottle wrapped in what appeared to be white gauze coated with hardened plaster of Paris.

"Help yourself, man. Great shit. Von Stiehls cherry wine all the way from the land of cheeseheads."

I took a long slash. The sickly-sweet taste brought back old high school memories of driving around the back roads of southern Wisconsin, listening to eight-track tapes of the Doors and Steppenwolf, and getting smashed on this wine, nonsense that was brewed up in Door Country northeast of Green Bay. Terrible wine but I drained the bottle on general principle.

"Man, I forgot to tell you, that stuff is laced with mescaline. You should get off like a rocket. Later, dude."

Later dude? I love snappy dialog. Mescaline? Christ. So much for my dream of writing flyfishing how-to books. I wandered among the gleeful throng. All friendly souls, probably gone on the Von Stiehls. As time passed so did what was left of my mind. A mescaline buzz in full regalia: everything was crystal clear but nothing made any sense. Par for the course, regardless of the state I'm in. I recognized Margo Timmins and the Cowboy Junkies' tune "Common Disaster," an appropriate piece of music, all things considered. Where was Margo when I needed her? Well, I had the feeling someone would pop up sooner or later. I realize that I'm in my mid-40s. Probably too old for this sort of silliness, but as a glamorous redheaded ex-companion, Ginny, once said, "John, when things get weird, let it slide." So I did, and I was feeling more than all right.

I wandered around with no serious intent, babbling away to anyone I bumped into. I had a great conversation with a yellow Lab about the fact that baseball was in serious trouble when managerial geniuses like Don Zimmer were still able to find employment. The dog agreed and then unleashed a diatribe about Dallas Green and his penchant for having the slowest man on the team try and steal second late in a blowout game. This went on for awhile, then I found myself being led into the woods by a pair of redheads. Believe me, I've had some experience in this area. Red hair means big trouble, bad craziness. And I was in the hands of two of them. Twins from the look of things. I was a dead man. But as Ginny said, let it slide.

I won't bore you with too many of the details: that they were wearing nothing but hip waders and Santa Fe Auto Body Express T-shirts; or that they each had the words "When life looks like easy street, there is danger at the door" tattooed just below their left shoulder blades in a circle with a coyote in the center. Or the fact that they were each five feet six and a half and extremely attractive: redheaded cheetahs. Portrait of a derelict writer as dead meat. At any rate I found myself standing knee-deep in the stream, casting a 2-weight and a Hornberg fly to cutthroat of six inches (or was it two feet?). Great fish that fluoresced as they leapt way above the glowing sapphire water. When the trout came to my feet the twins would drop to their knees and grab the fish and say, "Lay it down," before releasing the creature. This beat the hell out of fishing the Bighorn. Being arrested for not wearing a seatbelt beat fishing that river, come to think of it.

This went on for some time until we came to a mossy backside break in the proceedings. Things turned pleasurable in an obvious way with only one rule on their part: They did not like French kissing. "No tongue," they'd say. A bit frustrating but manageable. All the while during this tumultuous uproar, I kept thinking: I've got to write about this, but who will publish it? Never bothered me before. Why start now? I'd just finished a novella based on a real-life airline in the southwest that was nothing more than a front for drug running. I called it *Conquistador*. So why should I worry about detailing the craziness of redheads? Maybe this could serve as a warning to others. My life's work could be at hand. "Danger! Redhead on the horizon! Run for your very life! Pray for your soul!"

I must have drifted off somewhere, because when I came to, it was dark out. Stars by the billions filled the sky. I ricocheted off trees, rocks, and an occasional deer as I navigated by the sound of the Grateful Dead's "China Cat Sunflower." The party was in full swing. People whooping and hollering around giant bonfires. I drank some more wine, threw caution to the wind, and jumped and yelped with the best of them.

Sunrise came, the intense light burning my sensitized brain. I was sprawled next to Frank's truck. Frank was asleep on his front porch. Safe at home, I thought. What a night, if, indeed, there was such a night. I got up, stripped, and jumped in the river. The cold brought me around.

"How'd you like last night?" Frank asked when I returned.

"A fair effort."

"Thought we'd fish and take things easy. No gunfire today, eh John? They're all redheads when you look at it, aren't they?" and he was laughing pretty good. Frank knew more than he was letting on.

One hell of a valley.

There are other things I could tell you: such as the time Dizzy Trout went flyfishing for eagles with a Payne rod and Crazy Charlies, or the day Frank and I rolled a logging operation's D-9 down a mountainside. But that would be overkill. I kept this chapter in my life short for a reason: I could get busted for some of the stuff or, more likely, sent to the state hospital in Warm Springs. If you're really interested, you'll have to find the place and see for yourself. It's fine country, and if you are at all sincere, it will probably find you.

Epilogue

FOR ME TO SUGGEST THAT all of this actually happened would be a supreme stretch, a leap of the most exotic of faiths, even by my vaguely-defined standards. The nine tales are based on experiences, conjecture, wishful thinking, and a child's imagination. All of the characters have some basis in conventional reality but are actually an amalgam of traits gleaned from individuals encountered on the road fishing. There is a good deal more truth here than I originally thought there would be prior to writing; yet, the number of punches I pulled surprised me. Some of the idiots I wanted to rip apart, I ignored and pretended they never existed. Perhaps I've begun to mellow as old age and senility close in from the cold North.

The best explanation for these stories and how I approached writing them comes from Vollman in "A Note on the Truth of the Tales" at the end of *The Rainbow Stories*:

> Why should I care whether they are true or not? When someone tells me a story it is probably true for *him*; if not, why cannot I make it true for *me*? If I were perfect, I would believe everything I heard…If you object to my gullibility, I envy you; you will build great steel logic-castles, I am sure, whereas my roof has been leaking for three years.

Mine's been a sieve for close to 30, but who's counting? That's the point. Because of the perverse invasion of devices such as television, the Internet, global navigation systems we can carry in our shirt pockets, desktop computers with the capabilities to run countries—you name it—we've lost our sense of wonder, our ability to believe in dreams, to appreciate tall tales. The guides described here resemble those I have met over the years. The incidents are largely grounded in fact, but I took the liberty, as is my right, to twist and transform things into versions that pleased me in curious ways.

I'm sure a number of guides and outfitters will see themselves in here. To them, I rely once again on the words of another. This time, the late Frederick Exley in "A Note to the Reader" at the beginning of *A Fan's Notes*:

> Though the events in this book bear similarity to those of that long malaise, my life, many of the characters and happenings are creations solely of the imagination. In such cases, I of course disclaim any responsibility for their resemblance to real people or events…In creating such characters, I have drawn freely from the imagination and adhered only loosely to the pattern of my past life. To this extent, and for this reason, I ask to be judged as a writer of fantasy.

I love to fish and feel privileged to have made the friends I have, during times on the water or thereabouts, over the years. I enjoy telling stories, trying to make people believe what they normally wouldn't, in the hopes that the unbelievable may some day become true. If you see yourself in these words and find the representation objectionable, take a number and sue my ass. Relax, it's only an illusion anyway.

John Holt
Whitefish, Montana